THE BAR 10 BRAND

Madison Barton was the owner of the Diamond Garter Gaming House in the prosperous cattle town of McCoy, but all was not what it seemed, for Barton's real wealth came from cattle rustling. When he learned that Gene Adams had sent five hundred head of his prime Bar 10 longhorn steers to the auction pens at McCoy, it was a temptation the rustler could not resist. Trail boss Johnny Puma had to bring the herd through the narrow canyons of Deadman's Fork – an ideal place for an ambush. Johnny didn't stand a chance in hell of surviving – or did he?

THE BAR 10 BRAND

THE BAR 10 BRAND

by

Boyd Cassidy

Dales Large Print Books
Long Preston, North Yorkshire,
BD23 4ND, England.

British Library Cataloguing in Publication Data.

Cassidy, Boyd
    The Bar 10 brand.

A catalogue record of this book is
available from the British Library

ISBN   1-84262-339-7 pbk

First published in Great Britain 2003 by Robert Hale Limited

Copyright © Boyd Cassidy 2003

Cover illustration © Faba by arrangement with
Norma Editorial S.A.

Published in Large Print 2004 by arrangement with
Robert Hale Limited

Dales Large Print is an imprint of Library Magna Books Ltd.

Printed and bound in Great Britain by
T.J. (International) Ltd., Cornwall, PL28 8RW

Dedicated to Frank Copra Jr
with thanks

PROLOGUE

The Diamond Garter Gaming House was one of the few buildings within the boundaries of the cattle town of McCoy which had been constructed exclusively for those who enjoyed games of chance.

There were no dance-hall girls beneath its sloping roof and only those who paid a regular monthly membership fee were allowed to enter and enjoy the dubious pleasures of gambling in all its shapes and forms.

Here gamblers plied their trade and tried to milk the less competent men of their entire fortunes whilst drinking the finest whiskey and brandy.

But the Diamond Garter had many secrets hidden within its sturdy frame. For it had never been the profits from gambling that had allowed its owner to become one of the richest souls in the railhead town.

Madison Barton looked every inch the successful businessman from his tailored frock-coat to the gold jewellery he sported brashly. No man appeared more willing to display his wealth on his own tall frame than Barton. Gold cufflinks covered in cut diamonds hung from the sleeves of his handmade silk shirts and half his fingers bore rings that matched.

This was a man who gave everyone the impression that he was what he pretended to be, one of McCoy's leading figures.

But there were a few who knew the truth. Men who worked in and out of the exclusive gaming-house for the well-spoken Madison Barton. Men who did his bidding.

Those who played cards in the many highly decorated rooms that made up the Diamond Garter ought to have spotted the clues which were blatantly displayed for all to see. Gold seemed to be everywhere. The scores of large paintings that hung on the dark-red walls had frames covered in gold leaf, as were the sculptures which had been brought from the more civilized East.

And there was Barton himself who was never seen without thousands of dollars worth of the precious metal decorating his body and clothing.

The clues were all there but it seemed that the established authorities within McCoy were blind to them.

Madison Barton walked through the cloud of cigar smoke that filled his magnificent building and only paused to survey the men who were happily losing their fortunes on the turn of a card.

His hand turned the gleaming doorhandle and he entered his private office.

Sitting beneath the glowing oil-lantern, a solitary figure barely acknowledged the tall elegant man as he strode across the office towards the window. Barton pulled the heavy velvet drapes aside and stared out into the darkness and at the distant train that stood with its chimney smoking as hundreds of steers were being loaded into the cattle trucks behind the large engine tender.

'You missed that Lazy M herd, Flint,' Barton muttered in a low angry tone. 'Two hundred white-faced steers would have brought a tidy sum if you had been doing your job properly.'

'They slipped through, Madison,' Flint replied as he continued sipping at his drink. 'There ain't no telegraph down Adobe Falls way and we weren't given the information. By the time I heard of it, they were too close to McCoy for me to act.'

Madison Barton released the drape and then dragged his leather chair away from his desk. He pulled at the neat creases in his trousers before sitting down and staring straight into the face opposite him.

'Those steers would have brought us a tidy sum in the gold fields.'

Flint nodded.

'I know.'

Barton held his hands together as if in prayer and stared over the tips of his fingers at a man whose daring and cold-blooded disrespect for any other creature had made them both far wealthier than they ever needed to be.

'I imagine that we have to be realistic about it. We have to allow the majority of the herds to reach the auctioneers here at McCoy or someone might send for the army. That would stop us in our tracks.'

'Yep,' Flint agreed as he nursed his drink. 'One in ten is mighty fine when we get paid in gold-dust or nuggets.'

Barton smiled. It was not the smile of a man who was happy, it was the perverse smile of someone who liked to think about gold.

The owner of the Diamond Garter reached inside his coat, pulled out a large wallet and rested it upon the ink-blotter before him. He flicked open the large leather leaf and pulled out a hundred dollars in bills. He tossed them towards Flint.

'Keep the boys sweet, Flint,' Barton said.

Flint gathered up the money and quickly

pushed it into the breast pocket of his shirt.

'Sure enough.'

Then both men's attention was drawn to the side door to the dark unlit alley. It was being knocked at frantically.

'Open it,' Barton ordered as he rose to his feet.

Flint jumped from his chair, strode across the office and unlocked the door. He opened it and recognized the sweating face of Hec Smith the telegraph worker. The small man still had his black visor perched above his eyes as he was dragged in to the office.

'I got me some news, Mr Barton,' Smith said, waving a small scrap of paper in his hand at the elegant figure.

Madison Barton stepped from behind his desk and approached the smaller man with his hand outstretched.

'Give it to me, Hec.'

Smith handed the paper to the man who had paid him well over the years to supply him with vital information concerning cattle drives headed towards McCoy.

Barton looked at the note in his hand. It was nothing more than a series of dots and dashes.

'What's this say?'

Hec Smith ambled to the drinks tables, hesitantly poured himself a whiskey and downed it.

'It's real important, Mr Barton. Could mean thousands of dollars to you. Thousands of dollars in gold.'

'But what does it say?' Barton felt his temper rising. 'I pay you good money to bring me information. This is gibberish.'

'No, sir. It's telegraph shorthand. I reckon that you ought to pay me a lot more than you have been doing to translate that.'

Barton's eyes flashed at Flint, who was moving behind Smith.

'How much more?' Barton asked.

'I want a thousand bucks,' Hec Smith said quickly.

'A thousand dollars, you say?' Barton raised himself up to his full height. There was no sign of emotion in his face as he lifted his wallet from the desk and waved it in front of the little man who was trying to blackmail him. 'I think that I might have that sum in here.'

Smith moved closer as he watched the money being counted out before him in fifty-dollar bills.

'After all,' he said, 'I know a lot about what you critters have been up to, don't I? A thousand dollars is not too much to buy my silence.'

'Right enough, Hec,' Barton handed the bills to the sweating little figure. 'Now, tell me what the wire says.'

'It's from Gene Adams of the Bar 10 to the head auctioneer. He's sending five hundred head of prime longhorns up to McCoy but he ain't coming with them. They ought to be reaching the range below Deadman's Fork in a couple of days.'

Barton nodded. 'Who is leading the steers here?'

Smith pointed at the paper. 'He's sending

Johnny Puma in his place.'

Flint stepped up closer behind Smith and spoke over the man's shoulder. 'Johnny Puma is the young kid who rides for Adams.'

'Five hundred longhorns would bring a lot of gold over in the goldfields. A very valuable wire indeed,' Barton said as he signalled to Flint.

The long stiletto suddenly appeared in the right hand of Flint and its blade was thrust expertly into Hec Smith's back until it found the heart.

A look of horror etched the features of the telegraph worker as he suddenly realized that his pitiful existence was over. Before he hit the floor, Barton had plucked the money from his grasp and returned it to the wallet on his desk.

'That'll teach him not to try and blackmail me,' Barton said coldly. 'Well done, Flint. You are indeed an artist with that knife of yours.'

'What'll I do with the body, Madison?'

Barton waved a hand at his associate. 'Dump it in the alley somewhere.'

As Flint hauled the corpse up off the floor, he noticed that Barton was suddenly smiling again.

'Are we gonna try and dry gulch that herd, Madison?'

'An excellent idea. Five hundred head will do nicely.'

ONE

It was not the biggest herd that had made its way out of the Bar 10 over the years, but it was probably the most important. For times were hard across the Texan heartland. To the young rider whom Gene Adams had chosen to head the trail drive, it was his chance to prove that he had come of age.

Johnny Puma owed a debt to the rancher which he knew he could never repay, but he would never stop trying.

At last Johnny had been given the opportunity to prove that he was more than just another Bar 10 wrangler and could handle the responsibility of leading a trail drive without getting into trouble.

The 500 steers that Adams had placed in the care of the youthful rider were worth at least ten dollars a head and that money was needed badly.

The Bar 10, like all the lesser cattle ranches that spanned Texas had suffered its harshest summer for more than two decades and it had taken its toll. Half the stock had died long before the merciless sun had finally relented and allowed the much-required rain to rekindle life on the almost barren land. Many other ranchers had quit long before the drought had abated but not Adams.

For Gene Lon Adams was no quitter. This was his land and he was a Texan. True Texans would fight to their last drop of blood if that was what it took.

Gene Adams had worked hard to rebuild his depleted stock of longhorn steers once the rain had finally come back to his million-acre Bar 10.

It had taken nearly eighteen months to achieve, but eventually there were more than 3,000 steers roaming the lush Bar 10 ranges again, contentedly filling their bellies with sweet grass. But it had cost Adams nearly every cent he had managed to accumulate over the forty years since he had first settled the once untamed land and turned it into the vast Bar 10 ranch.

Now Adams had to try and sell at least a quarter of the famed Bar 10 longhorns to recoup his outlay and ensure the ranch went from strength to strength.

Johnny Puma knew that although his close friend would never admit it, Adams desperately needed money just to balance his books. The young cowboy, who had been a wanted outlaw before the rancher had given him refuge and a new name, would do anything rather than let his friend down.

For Gene Adams was more than just a friend, he was like the father that Johnny had never known.

Being put in charge of a herd to take to the railhead at the distant town of McCoy was an honour. One that he would not betray.

Johnny had set out with seventeen cowboys to control the 500 steers. A larger than average crew for the job, but it seemed that Adams was not taking any chances of losing even a single steer *en route*.

The camp-fire seemed to touch the stars above them as half the crew finished their supper from the back of the chuck wagon and headed back to the steers on the flat range that told the seasoned riders of the Bar 10 they were only two days away from their destination.

But this was no place to relax. This was a land of danger and every one of them knew it. Good grazing was sparse on this land, which was littered with box canyons. Ridges seemed to overlook every trail that led north towards McCoy and each boulder offered perfect cover for those who might wish to dry-gulch any innocent rider.

Johnny had felt uneasy for several hours before sundown as he had guided the herd. Even after night had fallen, he was still troubled.

No sooner had the full-bellied cowboys reached the herd for the three-hour night-guard duty, than their comrades rode into the temporary camp for their own supper.

Johnny Puma leapt off the saddle of his pinto pony and tied his reins to the running line where the dozen or more other horses were hitched. He released the cinch straps and hauled the heavy saddle off the back of the lathered-up pony before wiping it down. He then fed and watered the animal.

Johnny stared up at the sky as he walked towards the eating and sleeping cowboys gathered around the inviting fire. He un-buckled his chaps and dropped them down on the ground next to a large wheel of the chuck wagon before leaning on its tailgate.

'Hungry, Johnny?' Cookie asked as he

picked up a tin plate and headed for the stewpot that was hanging in the flames.

'Yep. And a tad thirsty too,' Johnny replied as he straightened up and tried to make his aching bones click back into place.

The large man known only as Cookie ladled out a huge portion of the stew on to the plate and then returned to the weary cowboy's side.

'That suit you?' Cookie asked, placing the plate on top of the wagon's tailgate as Johnny helped himself to a spoon from one of the many compartments at the rear of the wagon.

'Smells real good, Cookie.' Johnny smiled and started eating. 'Tastes kinda good too. What is it?'

'Chicken, I think.' Cookie grinned.

'What happened, did ya run out of diamond-back again?'

'I must be getting old, Johnny. I just can't catch them old rattlers like I used to.' The cook walked back to the camp-fire with a cup and then, using his apron to lift the heavy coffee-pot out of the flames, he poured a good measure of the black beverage.

'This coffee has got eggshells in it for body,' Cookie boasted.

'And sand?'

'Just a dash of sand.'

Johnny was so tired that he even found chewing a chore.

'I figure that we'll be at McCoy by noon the day after tomorrow.'

Cookie put the cup before the youthful trail boss and nodded in agreement.

'That's about the way I was figuring it, Johnny. We've made good time.'

Johnny Puma lifted the spoon from the sugar barrel and heaped the white crystals into his tin cup three times before he started stirring.

'That's a lotta sugar for you, Johnny,' Cookie noted.

'I need the energy, Cookie,' Johnny said, lifting the cup and carefully sipping from it.

The older, wiser man, who obviously enjoyed his own cooking as much as any of the men he kept well fed during the long trail drive yawned as he rested his rear on an empty box. His fingers found a primed pipe and placed its stem between his teeth.

'You ought to rest more, son.'

Johnny finished his stew and dropped the plate in a bucket of soapy water. He sighed heavily and then sat on the ground next to the cook with his coffee cupped in his hands.

'Gene is relying on me to get these steers to McCoy,' the young cowboy said through the steam that rose from the tin cup. 'I can't let him down. It's too important.'

'He wouldn't want you to kill yourself, Johnny,' Cookie said, striking a match with his thumbnail and sucking its flame into the pipe bowl. 'I reckon that you've been pushing yourself too hard. You have to rest, boy.'

Johnny sipped at the coffee again. 'I just don't want to let him down. This is the first time he's given me the responsibility of leading a drive. I know that the Bar 10 needs the money that these longhorns will bring. I just have to do my best. I can't let him down.'

'You get a few hours' shut-eye,' Cookie said through the smoke that drifted from his mouth.

'I ain't sleepy.'

'You sure are,' Cookie argued. 'These boys need a trail boss who is alert. They ain't got a brain between the bunch of them and need you to do their thinking for them. What good is a boss who is too tuckered out to think straight?'

Johnny knew the older man was right.

'OK. I'll get my bedroll and try and catch me a few hours' sleep.'

Cookie smiled. 'You'll be all the better for it. A man that's tired can make mistakes and that's one thing that I reckon you don't wanna do.'

'Damn right,' the youngster agreed. 'I ain't gonna win no popularity contest back on the Bar 10 if I make a hash of this job.'

'Gene Adams knows that you can handle

this, Johnny,' Cookie added. 'I'd think of it as an honour, 'coz in all the years that I've known him, I ain't never seen him send out a herd of this size without him being at the head of it on that old chestnut mare of his.'

Johnny rose to his feet and placed the tin cup down on the tailgate. He stared across at his friend Happy Summers who was snoring his head off propped up against his saddle next to the camp-fire. The other men were all dozing off until it was time for them to ride night guard on the herd once more.

'Happy never has any trouble sleeping,' Johnny observed.

'He don't have no trouble eating either,' Cookie added. 'I reckon he had three plates of stew before you got to camp.'

Johnny looked at the other men.

'I sure wish that old Tomahawk was here. I miss that old coyote.'

Cookie laughed. 'Yep, I reckon it ain't the same on a trail drive without that old grumbler.'

Johnny stretched his arms until he felt his

bones settling back into place. 'I just hope that I can get to sleep.'

'You could always count sheep,' Cookie puffed.

The young cowboy leaned down to the cook and winked.

'You know better than to say that to a cattleman, Cookie. Shame on you.'

Cookie was still smiling when he watched the young man crawling into his trail blanket beside the other sleeping cowboys. Then his eye drifted down to the silver hunter watch in his hand. He would wake them all in three hours so that they could relieve the other cowboys riding night guard.

TWO

Sam Flint was a man who knew how to get anything he wanted and what he wanted was heading straight towards him. His spies had already informed him that 500 head of prime Bar 10 longhorn steers were on the hoof and being driven towards the railhead at McCoy.

For more than five years he and his hand-picked team of rustlers had taken on and defeated lesser cattlemen than the famed Gene Adams and his riders of the Bar 10. But now Sam Flint had been informed that the seemingly ageless white-haired Adams was not leading this trail drive. The odds were now in Flint's favour and he knew it.

Without Gene Adams, there was more than a good chance of snatching the entire herd from the cowboys and wranglers who were bringing them to McCoy.

As soon as he heard the news, Flint had rounded up nearly thirty hardened rustlers and promised them that he would share fifty per cent of whatever he managed to get for the herd, if they did exactly as he instructed.

There were a lot of men who were hungry in northern Texas and willing to do anything to fill their pockets and their bellies.

The troop of riders headed south-west to intercept the trail drive, which they knew was nearing the thriving railhead town of McCoy.

When you went up against the Bar 10, you were dicing with trouble, but Flint had never been one to shy away from trouble. It had been his only companion for more than three decades. He had stolen practically everything in his time and had always made a handsome profit.

But to take Bar 10 steers with their unique brand was not something that even professional rustlers did without a great deal of thought.

Flint knew that the Bar 10 was well known in McCoy and it would be impossible to take the herd there. But he had no intention of running the well-fed steers anywhere close to any cattle town.

That would be too risky.

Stealing cattle was as serious a crime as horse theft. It was a hanging offence. When you stole anything with legs on it in Texas you had to make sure that you had a guaranteed market before you started.

Sam Flint had that market already well established.

He liked his neck far too much to risk having it stretched by any lawman's rope. His was a far more subtle plan. Flint had already used it many times when dealing with far smaller herds from less powerful ranches.

Flint would not try to sell any branded steers at legitimate cattle auctions.

His established customers were the hundreds of hungry men who were working their claims in the goldfields that dotted the northern ridges along the New Mexico border. No one knew exactly how many men were in the mountains, spending their lives armed with pickaxes as they searched for the elusive golden ore that had a way of possessing a man's soul.

The prospectors had little time to waste by deserting their valuable claims to go searching for goods and food. What they wanted was brought to them by men like Flint. Men who knew how to get top dollar for anything and everything they traded.

The gold-miners would pay in gold-dust for fresh meat and never ask a single question. They did not ask for proof of ownership. They were just grateful to have something besides prairie chicken to eat.

Flint had already established himself in the territories as someone who could provide top-grade beef on the hoof. So there was no problem selling the steers once they were driven into the untamed mountains.

The only problem that faced Flint was working out how he would get such a large herd there, once it was stolen. It was a far bigger job than any of his previous ones.

Five hundred steers took a lot of handling and that was why he had gathered so many experienced cattlemen around him this time. He knew that for the odds to be in his favour there had to be at least a half-dozen men used to handling the unpredictable longhorns within the ranks of his thirty deadly henchmen.

Up until now, Flint had managed to scare most of the cowboys whom he and his men attacked on the smaller trail drives, but he knew that the Bar 10 men were not like those from other cattle ranches.

They had the reputation of fighting to the death when Adams was leading them, but Adams was not leading them this time. Would his absence stack the odds even more in Flint's favour? The question ran through his mind.

The thirty riders trailed Sam Flint along the rim of the great Sioux mesa. Yet no one could see the dust that rose from the hoofs of their mounts beneath the dark star-filled sky. These men were used to travelling unseen during the hours of darkness.

They were a force to be reckoned with.

The main core of the men whom Flint had hired in and around McCoy were skilled gunmen. Men who would kill if ordered to do so, and were more than likely to do so of their own free will should the mood take them.

Sam Flint knew that the miners in the goldfields would willingly pay ten times the price that Gene Adams would get at auction in McCoy for his precious longhorns.

Had Flint chosen to trade legal provisions with the isolated mining camps, he would have become a rich man long ago. But, as with so many compulsive thieves, he seemed to spend all his time and energy finding ways of stealing things which belonged to law-abiding others.

That meant a huge profit for the beady-eyed rider who led his army of followers ever closer to the box canyons and massive boulders of Deadman's Fork. Sam Flint was the sort of man who could have become successful in any profession he had chosen to follow. He was intelligent and greedy and that had ensured that he chose to ride on the wrong side of the law.

Flint led his followers on. They had to reach their goal long before the unsuspecting Bar 10 wranglers drove the large herd into the place that had been designed by nature as a perfect spot to ambush the unwary.

They would ride throughout the night in order to set their trap. Once they reached Deadman's Fork, they could make certain that none of the Bar 10 riders would get out of the maze of smooth rocks alive.

Flint drove on at the head of his small army.

THREE

It was still only half-way through the long cool night and yet the night guards had been changed for the third time. The weary riders who had spent the previous few hours circling the sleeping 500 longhorns were now heading back to camp whilst their replacements slowly took over their positions as quietly as possible. Each of the Bar 10 cowboys knew that the one thing that you had to avoid at all costs was spooking the massive steers.

For when longhorns stampeded, people died.

This was the last shift of the night and would take them into sunrise and beyond. But none of the riders liked tending the herd as night gave way to day. Tricks of the light had been known to confuse even the calmest of herds. It was a time when the riders had to be extra vigilant.

But there were still another few hours before dawn.

Happy Summers' instincts were well-honed after so many years riding for the Bar 10. He had only just ridden out from the night-camp after four hours' sleep when he spotted something to the north that made the hairs on his neck rise beneath the tightly knotted bandanna.

The well-proportioned wrangler drew in his reins hard as he stood in his stirrups and gazed out through the moonlight across the heads and horns of the bedded-down steers.

The steam that rose off the backs of 500 cattle had a tendency to confuse even the keenest of eyes. Happy sat back on his saddle, pulled out his tobacco pouch and started to roll himself a smoke. He was puzzled.

Johnny Puma rode up behind his thoughtful friend atop his pinto pony and reined in.

'What's wrong, Happy? You look like you

seen a ghost or something?'

Happy turned in his saddle. He pushed the brim of his battered hat off his brow and ran tongue across the gummed paper of his cigarette. The look on his face was pure puzzlement.

'Could have been ghosts, I reckon. Take a look yonder, Johnny.' Happy pointed at the distant ridge that lay between them and their eventual destination. 'I might be still dreamin', but I'd swear that I seen riders.'

Johnny Puma swung the pinto around until it was aimed in the direction that Summers was indicating. He screwed up his eyes and tried to see through the steam that rose off the backs of the 500 hundred head of longhorns.

'Are you sure?'

Happy could hear the doubt in his friend's voice. He placed the cigarette between his lips and struck a match with his thumbnail. He inhaled deeply.

'Nope, I ain't sure at all, Johnny. But I could have sworn that I seen riders skimming the top of that ridge and then disappearing down towards Deadman's Fork.'

At any other time Johnny would not have given the worries of his fellow-wrangler a second thought, but this drive was different. This time he was responsible for the whole thing and could not afford to take risks.

'How many riders do you think you saw?' Johnny asked. He leaned across from his own saddle until his gloved hand was resting on Happy's buckskin gelding's neck.

'Heck, I ain't even sure that I seen riders at all now.' Happy shrugged as smoke drifted through his teeth.

Johnny gave the herd a fleeting glance then turned his gaze in to the eyes of the larger man.

'I've known you for too long to believe that them peepers of yours could make that kinda mistake, even at night,' Johnny said thoughtfully. 'If you think that you saw something, I'd bet a month's wages that you did.'

Happy Summers frowned doubtfully. 'It

might just have been a trick of the light, or a breeze kicking up some dust. I ain't fully awake yet. I don't wanna get you fretting for nothing, Johnny.'

Johnny Puma released his grip on the black mane of his pal's mount and straightened up.

'There ain't been no breeze for days, Happy. You say that you saw dust on that ridge and so did I.'

'Then you figure I could be right?'

Johnny nodded. 'Yep. I reckon you saw riders OK. And they're headed for Deadman's Fork. That would be a darn good place for a bushwhacking.'

Happy rubbed his face with his bandanna. 'Dry-gulchers?'

'Maybe. There's only one way to find out for sure.' The young rider stood in his stirrups and hauled the pinto around as his keen eyes surveyed the land around the flat fertile range. His mind kept repeating the same question, over and over again.

What would Gene do?

Johnny realized that he would have to live another thirty-five years before he knew the answer to that nagging question. Until then, he alone had to make the decisions.

'Do you think there are enough men riding night-guard if we take us a little diversion, Happy?' he queried as he thought about riding to Deadman's Fork to investigate.

'Reckon so.'

Johnny glanced back at the camp-fire beyond the chuck wagon where the rest of his crew were resting. He could not ask them to saddle up their horses to ride with him and he dare not take the night guards away from their duties of keeping the testy herd in check.

'You up to a long ride, Happy?' Johnny asked.

Happy raised an eyebrow.

'I guess so. Why?'

Johnny's eyes narrowed as he gazed at the distant ridge bathed in moonlight.

'I just thought that we'd take us a look-see before we drive this herd into that perfect spot for an ambush.'

'Do you actually think that some *hombres* would try and dry-gulch this herd, Johnny?'

'We ain't gonna find out sitting here talking, are we?'

Happy Summers gathered his reins in his skilled hands and then tapped his spurs into the sides of his mount. The buckskin quietly picked up pace until it was alongside the trotting pinto pony.

Both riders stood in their stirrups as they headed straight for the mist-covered hills.

FOUR

Gene Lon Adams lifted the heavy saddlebags on to the back of his chestnut mare and tied them securely to the cantle. The army always paid in gold coin. It was one reason he had always liked doing business with them. He touched the brim of his black ten-gallon hat to the officer and then stepped into his stirrup and pulled himself on to the Texan saddle.

The rancher gathered in the slack of his reins with his black-gloved hands and watched as his ancient friend, Tomahawk, ambled out of the army garrison, grumbling.

'A fine state of affairs when a man can't even get himself steak dinner just 'coz they can't find some *hombre* to cook the darn thing.'

'Quit belly-aching, Tomahawk.' Adams chuckled at his friend.

'That's the trouble, Gene. My belly is aching.' Tomahawk scratched his beard, stepped down from the boardwalk of the garrison headquarters and dragged his reins free of the hitching pole. 'And another thing, why are we heading out in the middle of the night?'

'Because I say we are, that's why.' Adams smiled.

'I'm powerful hungry, Gene,' Tomahawk complained as he mounted his black cutting horse. 'I wanna eat a steak. I'm sick of beans and hardtack. How come we bring a hundred longhorns all the way to this darn fort and we don't get us to eat a steak dinner before heading back to the Bar 10?'

'You'll get a steak dinner as soon as we get home.' Gene laughed. 'What's really bothering you?'

'I'm a tad confused, Gene. I don't get it. How come we hired all them halfwits to help us bring these steers here?' Tomahawk asked, his beard jutting out at his friend.

Adams smiled as he watched the old-timer turn his horse around to face the open military gate.

'Look, Tomahawk. This job was fast money. That's why we hired a handful of drovers to help us get the hundred head here without using what's left of our Bar 10 boys. They have to look after the ranch. With Johnny taking most of our best Bar 10 cowboys to McCoy with him, and Fort Grant wiring us for beef, what else could we have done? You know the fix the ranch has been in over the last year or so.'

Tomahawk nodded and smiled a toothless grin at his oldest friend.

'How much did them steers bring?'

'Five hundred dollars profit after paying off them drovers.'

'Is that good?'

'It'll help, old-timer. It'll help.'

Tomahawk adjusted the Indian hatchet in his belt and tapped his boots against the sides of the gelding. The horse gathered pace beside the taller chestnut. The two riders cantered out of the fort and headed through the darkness along the dusty trail that they had used to guide them over the latter part of their trail drive.

Adams stared up at the moon and then back at his friend. He pulled back on his reins and brought his horse to a stop. The old-timer swung his mount around and looked at his companion. Even in the light of the moon, Tomahawk could see the troubled expression on Gene Adams's face.

'OK, Gene. Spit it out. What's gnawing at

ya craw?'

Adams looked at his pal. 'I just had me a real bad feeling, Tomahawk.'

'Ya still worried about Johnny?'

'Reckon I am.' Adams gritted his teeth and looked to the north. 'How far from McCoy do you figure we are?'

Tomahawk edged his black gelding closer to the troubled cattleman.

'It ain't far from here if'n we cut across the old Adobe Flats desert. Once ya get across that desert, McCoy is no more than five miles north.'

Adams raised an eyebrow. 'Do you know the way there from here, old-timer?'

Tomahawk's beard bristled. 'You bet. I've ridden that trail a hundred times.'

Gene Adams nodded. 'Then I guess that one more time wouldn't hurt none, would it?'

'Johnny might get a mite angry if he thinks ya checking up on him, Gene.' Tomahawk shrugged. 'He might think ya don't trust him to get the job done.'

'We'll not interfere. We'll just be there in the background in case he needs us.' Gene Adams pulled the gloves tight on his hands.

'If I ever get myself into trouble I'm sure that you'll be there to help me as well, Gene.' Tomahawk chuckled.

Adams leaned over and tugged the jutting beard of the old-timer.

'Not hardly. You're always in trouble. I'd waste my entire life.'

Both men spurred their mounts and headed north towards the Adobe Flats desert.

FIVE

Johnny Puma and Happy Summers made good time as they steered their mounts toward the outcrop of gigantic boulders. Deadman's Fork was well named and both men knew it. It was a place where many men had met their end at the hands of Sam Flint and his followers.

The brilliant moon above them rained its glowing, haunting light over the entire untamed region, making it impossible for them to find cover. There was no way that they could have approached Deadman's Fork unnoticed and both men knew it. If there was anyone there, they would have spotted Johnny and Happy out on the flat range long ago.

Neither rider had spoken since leaving the herd miles behind them and both would have remained silent if it had not been for the fact that once again Happy noticed something on the rocky horizon.

He reached across and grabbed at the bridle of his friend's pony. He hauled it back, at the same time reining in his buckskin.

Both horses came to a stop as their masters wondered whether to continue their advance.

'What is it?' Johnny Puma asked the wrangler who stared ahead of them worriedly.

Happy bit his lip and pointed at the moonlit boulders which rose heavenward before them.

'Watch that crag at the top of the ridge, Johnny.'

Johnny did as he was instructed. For nearly a minute he saw nothing. Then his eyes caught a fleeting glimpse of the reason Happy was looking so terrified.

The flash of metal caught in the bright light of the moon seemed like a beacon.

'See it?' Happy asked.

'Yep, I seen it,' Johnny replied. He stood in his stirrups and tried to see more.

'What ya reckon it was?'

'Either the metal sights or magazine of a Winchester, Happy.'

The older man shook his head and sighed heavily. He did not like the sound of Johnny's words one bit. He was no gunfighter and used his own gun to hammer nails into fence posts. When it came to firing the Colt, he barely knew which end to aim with.

'That means we got us a reception committee waiting for us, Johnny.' Happy tried to swallow but his throat had suddenly gone as dry as a cactus.

'Seems like it,' Johnny mumbled. His eyes traced the vast array of rocks that loomed over the pass through which they usually brought their cattle on the way to McCoy.

'I ain't no gunfighter, Johnny.' Happy's voice croaked nervously as his hands fumbled with his reins. 'I don't wanna get into no fight with nobody. 'Specially if'n they're good with their own guns. I'm just a cowboy. I couldn't hit anybody with my gun even if I was standing two feet away from him.'

Johnny glanced briefly at his friend.

'Don't fret none, Happy. They'll probably kill ya with their first shot. You might not even feel a thing.'

Happy's head swung until he was looking straight at Johnny. 'Now ya joshing me, ain't ya?'

Johnny returned his attention to the rocks.

'Try to stop sweating, Happy. Your horse might get himself drowned otherwise.'

Happy Summers gave out a huge frustrated sigh. He knew that if there was one man you wanted beside you when trouble broke out, it was the young man called Johnny Puma. For unlike himself or most of the other Bar 10 riders, Johnny had started his life travelling a very different trail. Happy had heard stories in the bunkhouse that Johnny Puma, who was still only somewhere in his twenties, had once been a wanted outlaw. Then he had had the good fortune to meet Gene Adams.

Adams had given him a home and a new name. It was said that the only time that Adams ever lied, was when the law asked questions concerning the young man who rode the pinto pony. Yet even though he had left that life behind him, Johnny had never lost any of his skills with his six-shooters.

With Johnny Puma on your side, you had a better than average chance of survival.

Happy looked down at the matched pair

of Colt .45s that rested in their hand-tooled holsters and knew that the stories were all true. No ordinary cowboy ever sported a shooting rig like that. The only men who did were those who knew how to use their weaponry.

Johnny pointed. 'Look, Happy. Another one.'

'Let's get out of here before they see us.'

'They saw us coming a mile or so back, Happy.' Johnny said bluntly as he flicked the safety loop off one of his prized Colts.

Happy mopped the sweat from his face with the end of his bandanna. 'Then how come they ain't opened up with them Winchesters of theirs yet?'

'Two reasons,' Johnny replied calmly. 'The first is that they don't want us to be put off from bringing the herd through the pass and the second reason is, we're out of range.'

There was little comfort in the words for the troubled wrangler as he vainly tried to sit still in his saddle.

'That's dandy. So what'll we do next?'

Johnny rubbed his chin thoughtfully.

'I ain't too sure,' he admitted.

Happy Summers felt his jaw drop. 'But you have to know what to do next, Johnny. You're the trail boss. You make the decisions and the rest of us follow them. Ya can't just sit there and say that ya don't know what to do. It ain't right. I bet that Gene would know what to do.'

Johnny shook his head.

'I mean, I ain't decided what to do yet.'

Happy nodded. 'Phew, that makes me feel a lot more confident. You take ya time. I'll have me a drink of water and you just figure all this out.'

Johnny watched as his friend lifted the canteen from the saddle horn and un-screwed its stopper.

'You OK?'

'Nope I ain't OK, at all. I'm having me a little moment of real bad nerves.'

Johnny Puma smiled as he watched most of the canteen's water spilling down his companion's shirt front before it reached the wrangler's mouth.

'I could send you into them rocks with guns blazing.'

Happy choked on his water as he tried to say something.

'Or I could give you my trusty carbine and make ya give me cover as I go in there with both my Colts blazing.' Johnny laughed.

'Ya ain't serious, are ya?' Happy gulped. 'All you've left out is for me and you to surround the varmints.'

The look of horror carved into Happy's features made Johnny forget the danger that lay ahead for a few brief seconds.

'Whatever we do is gonna cost us, Happy,' Johnny said. 'Either time, money or the lives of some of those boys back there at the herd.'

Happy knew that the statement was probably true.

Johnny pulled back on his reins and turned his pony until it was facing the distant light of their camp-fire. He knew that whoever was lying in wait for their herd would not allow any of them to leave the pass alive, once they had entered with the cattle. Suddenly the full weight of responsibility began to weigh the handsome young cowboy down. He knew that he had to come up with a solution to their problem.

'You thought of something yet, Johnny?' Happy asked.

Johnny's eyes flashed across the distance between them. 'Yep, but you ain't gonna like it.'

SIX

Sam Flint moved through the boulders until he was at the highest point. From here, he had a totally unobstructed view of the range below them. He could see the distant camp-fire and the sleeping herd. But most of all he could see the two stationary riders. Flint moved next to his most lethal hired gun and rested his belly across the smooth rocks next to him.

'They still ain't moved,' Flint noted curiously as his eyes focused on Happy and Johnny.

'You thinking what I'm thinking, Sam?' Bodine Bonny asked. He clutched on to his Winchester and continued watching the two horsemen who seemed to be neither continuing their approach or retreating to their herd.

'I'm starting to think that they've seen us,' Flint responded sharply. 'And you?'

Bonny spat at the ground.

'Yeah, that's what I was thinking OK.'

Flint turned and looked at the men he had secreted in the high boulders of the notorious Deadman's Fork. They were waiting just as he had told them to wait.

Waiting for the kill.

'I reckon that we might be wrong, though.'

Bonny spat again. He laid his rifle on the boulder and searched his pockets for his block of chewing-tobacco. His grubby hands found the black block and lifted it to his brown stained teeth. He took a large bite and chewed feverishly.

'You could be right. They might just be scouting to check out the best route for the herd through the pass.'

'Those Bar 10 riders are not as dumb as most of the cowboys we're used to dry-gulching.' Flint sighed heavily. 'I reckon that must be why old Gene Adams has survived so long.'

'What if they decide to take another route into McCoy?' Bonny asked.

'The only other way to McCoy from here is out across the desert.' Flint almost smiled. 'There ain't a drop of water out there.'

Bonny said nothing, just spat again.

Suddenly, Flint raised an eyebrow as he watched the pair of riders. He recognized the pinto pony and knew that it belonged to the man whom everyone called Johnny Puma. Puma was someone who was a match for any of the hired killers he had with him.

'You ever met Johnny Puma, Bodine?' Flint asked the brooding killer.

Bonny spat another black lump of spittle at the ground.

'Nope. I never even heard of the critter. Why?'

'It ain't important.' Sam Flint pushed himself up from the boulder and then rubbed the corners of his mouth. His mind raced as he wondered why the two riders were holding their horses in check. Why had they stopped advancing? Had they seen him and his men? Would the Bar 10 men actually bring the herd of longhorns through the pass?

So many questions. But no answers.

'We can't do anything but wait, Bodine,' Flint said at last, angrily.

'I'm good at waiting.'

'I know that. The trouble is, are the rest of the new boys as good at it as you?' Flint was worried about the extra men he had hired for this job. 'I'll have to try and keep them sweet.'

'Yep. I wondered why ya brought them bottles of rye along,' Bonny said. He spat once more. 'Reckon with a bellyful of whiskey, they'll be sweet enough. Then all we have to do is just wait and see if them cowboys decide to bring them longhorns into the pass.'

'They will. They have to,' Flint said. 'Even if they suspect that we're here, they have to get them steers to McCoy.'

Bonny spat again.

Flint stared up at the sky. The moon seemed to be taunting them all.

'They won't be able to move that herd until dawn at the earliest. You better try and get some shut-eye. I'll tell the rest of the boys to do the same.'

Bodine Bonny grunted. 'I'll just keep chewing, Sam. I ain't in the mood to sleep. I'm in the mood to kill.'

Flint began to move through the boulders again. 'It's up to you, Bodine.'

'That it is.' Bonny continued chewing and

watching the riders who were just out of range of his powerful carbine. The gunman knew that he dare not fire any of his weapons until the cattle were within the narrow pass anyway. This was a waiting game and he was an expert at it.

When you made your living by ambushing men, you got used to waiting.

SEVEN

The desert sprawled out around the two riders as they drove their mounts across its rock-hard sun-baked surface at top speed. The sound of the cracking sand echoed all about them as the horses' hoofs pounded ceaselessly on and on. The large yellow moon in the cloudless sky gave everything an eerie appearance, but neither horseman noticed. All they could think about was getting to the other side of this hellish place.

The riders knew that they had only a few hours before the sun rose above the horizon, bringing with it the blistering heat that had claimed so many lives in the past.

Both men knew that if they were caught out on this arid landscape in the day, they would not survive long. This was a place where not one drop of water had ever been discovered.

Unlike other places that the two original Bar 10 men had ventured into over the years, this was a land where the living were easily destroyed.

This desert had a thousand ways to kill.

Ahead in the distance, the moonbeams highlighted the ridge that was made up of huge boulders. They seemed to have been stacked by some unseen gigantic hand. Both horsemen knew that Deadman's Fork lay within the maze of trails that wove through the mountainous region. Beyond that, the town of McCoy and its railhead beckoned to all cattle ranchers. It was possible to avoid the infamous pass that led into Deadman's Fork and ride straight through the desert to McCoy, but it was risky. Two riders might be able to make it if they were carrying extra canteens filled with precious water, but no one had ever managed to drive a herd of steers across this desert.

Cattle had a habit of eating anything that strayed in front of their insatiable mouths as they were driven ever forward and the only things that grew in this desert were poisonous. Only riders had a chance of keeping their mounts' noses away from the sparse, lethal vegetation.

Tomahawk reined in his black quarter horse until at last it stopped. The tall chestnut mare was slowed by Gene Adams beside the bearded old-timer until it too came to a halt.

Adams watched as Tomahawk slid from his saddle and tried to catch his breath. His wrinkled eyes were screwed up and staring at their eventual goal.

'What's wrong, Tomahawk?' Adams asked, dismounting to take the weight off his horse's shoulders.

Tomahawk lifted his canteen from the saddle horn and began to turn its stopper.

'How good are them eyes of yours, Gene?'

Adams knew that his old friend's eyesight was far from what it had once been. He also knew how sensitive the old-timer could become about the subject.

'They ain't as good as they were when I was twenty. Why?' The rancher laughed.

'Are we still headed for Deadman's Fork?' Tomahawk took a long swallow of the cold liquid. 'We should be headed straight for the biggest boulder that's balanced up on top of all the smaller ones. Are we headed for it?'

Adams rested a gloved hand on the skinny shoulder. 'Straight and true, Tomahawk. You're right on course, as always.'

The words comforted the man who had always seemed old in appearance if not in spirit.

'Good. I was starting to get confused with the moonlight and all.' Tomahawk sighed.

The tall broad-shouldered rancher removed his own canteen from the saddle and unscrewed its stopper. He could see Tomahawk looking all around them at the moonlit sand. The rancher knew that even if his eyesight was not what it had once been, he was still the finest tracker he had ever known. But they were not tracking anything out here in the desert, Adams thought.

'What you looking for, Tomahawk?'

'Critters, Gene. Ya knows I don't like them crawling biting critters that like this kinda land,' Tomahawk replied. His tongue rotated around his whiskers.

'Do you mean scorpions?' Adams teased.

Tomahawk shuddered. 'Don't ya start talking about scorpions again, Gene. Ya knows that I can't stand them evil little critters at the best of times.'

Adams knew that his friend's fear was based on good sense. This desert had countless ways of killing and none of them was pretty.

'We ought to get to McCoy a couple of hours after sunrise, I reckon. What do you think?'

Tomahawk watched as his friend took a single swallow of his water.

'That's about the way I figured it but I'm a tad worried.'

Adams lowered his canteen from his mouth and stared down at his companion.

'Worried? What about?'

The bony hand shook the canteen. It sounded half-empty.

'We need to get us some water long before we reach McCoy, Gene. Once we water these horses, we'll be dry. And this ain't no land to be riding across when ya dry.'

The rancher knew exactly what his friend meant. 'What do you suggest?'

'The closest water is in Deadman's Fork. I reckon we could reach there before sun-up.'

Gene Adams removed his large black hat and dropped it on the sand between his horse's forelegs. He poured the remainder of his water into it. The moonlight made his hair seem even whiter than it was.

'Then we had better head for the pass at Deadman's Fork, old-timer.' Adams nodded as his friend pulled his own hat off his head and lay it carefully in front of the black gelding. He poured all his water into it. It was a task that did not take long.

Tomahawk nodded slowly as he ran a finger along the lip of the canteen and sucked the last of its moisture into his toothless mouth.

'We might run into Johnny and the boys.'

Adams smiled. 'We ought to get there before he does.'

'How do ya figure that, Gene?'

'Johnny knows better than to get a herd up on its feet before dawn, don't he?'

'Yeah, that's right. We taught him good.'

Gene Adams replaced the stopper on his canteen and then hung it over the saddle horn. He knew that he had given the young cowboy his biggest challenge by making him trail boss of this cattle drive. He knew that if Johnny were to even see him and old Tomahawk it would make the youngster think that they did not trust him to get the job done.

'I sure hope that we can get into the pass and head on to McCoy before Johnny and the boys reach there with the herd.'

Tomahawk could read his friend's mind.

'Yeah, it would look like we was snooping on them.'

'The last thing Johnny needs is to think that we're nursemaiding him, old-timer.' Adams plucked his Stetson off the ground and placed it back on his head. The cool droplets of water that traced down his neck felt good.

'Johnny would get riled up for sure.' Tomahawk laughed.

'And we don't want the young 'un riled, do we?'

'Nope. He's bad enough when he's happy.'

'True. Very true.' Adams smiled.

Tomahawk leaned down and picked up his damp hat.

'If'n we ride hard and fast, we'll get through the pass before Johnny and the rest of them boys wakes up.'

'I reckon you're right.'

Tomahawk's eyes twinkled in the moon-light. 'Heck, Gene. Ain't ya figured out after all the years we've been together, that I'm always right?'

'I'm too tired to argue,' Adams said, tugging the jutting beard of his pal. 'Let's ride.'

The two men mounted their refreshed horses and drove on towards the distant ridge. This desert was no place to be in when you were dry.

EIGHT

Johnny Puma watched his men eating their breakfast one after another from beside the chuck wagon. He had stood silently, like a marble statue, as Cookie had dished up the eggs and biscuits on to the tin plates of the Bar 10 men.

The young trail boss had set about waking

up each of the sleeping men as soon as he and Happy had ridden back into their temporary camp.

Each of the cowboys knew that Johnny had something in mind and yet not a single one of them had asked him what it was.

They just ate their meals and then mounted up and returned to the still sleeping herd.

As the last of them had been served his food, Cookie turned and looked at the ashen-faced youngster. His eyes fixed on Johnny.

'What's going on, Johnny?'

For a moment there was no reply as the trail boss watched the last of the riders mounting up and joining the rest of their comrades on the range. As the dust off the horses' hoofs began to settle, Johnny glanced at the cook.

'I'm thinking of doing something that you might consider a mite loco, Cookie.'

'I'm game. Go on.' Cookie leaned closer to the cowboy.

'Me and Happy know that there are riflemen up in the crags overlooking the pass into Deadman's Fork. We counted at least a dozen of them but there might be more.'

Cookie straightened up and frowned.

'Dry-gulchers?'

Cookie pulled out his pipe and chewed its stem as he pondered the thought of there being men lying in wait for them. If there was one thing that he disliked above all others, it was dry-gulchers. To him, they were just back-shooters and lower than the lowest creatures that dwelled in Hell itself.

'What are you intending to do that's so loco?' the cook asked.

Johnny gave a huge sigh and rested both his gloved hands on the tailgate of the chuck wagon. His eyes stared down at the flour-covered top that still showed the imprint of the dozens of fresh-rolled biscuits the cook had prepared for their breakfast.

'I'm thinking of driving the herd straight into the pass at stampede pace. Straight down their throats.'

Cookie struck a match on the seat of his pants and sucked its flame into the bowl of his pipe. As smoke billowed from his mouth he said nothing. His face was totally still, as if he were afraid to show any emotion.

'Drive the entire herd into the pass, you say?'

Johnny nodded but did not take his eyes off the flour-covered tailgate.

'Yep. Drive them as fast as the boys can make them run.'

Cookie also nodded.

'Sounds pretty loco.'

'That's what I was figurin', but I'm damned if I can think of anything else to get us out of this fix.' Johnny sighed heavily as if a ton-weight was resting on his young shoulders.

'This is sure a pretty bad state of affairs, and no mistake,' Cookie said. He removed the stem of the pipe from his mouth and looked at the smoke that trailed from it. 'But stamping a herd of five hundred long-horns is a mighty risky business. Do you think that you can control them once they get a head of steam under their rawhide bellies, Johnny?'

The young cowboy raised an eyebrow. 'I've tried to think of another way but there ain't one as far as I can figure.'

'What are the other choices?' Cookie asked, pressing the burning tobacco ash down into the pipe bowl with his thumb.

Johnny stood upright and brushed the flour from his gloves.

'I thought about us taking the herd to McCoy by going into the desert, but Gene always said that all the vegetation out there is real poisonous. Then I thought about us holding up here until them bushwhacking varmints got tired and headed for home, but the herd has already eaten all the grazing. There also ain't enough water on this range and after a few hours them longhorns are gonna smell the water up in the pass and we'd not be able to control them.'

Cookie puffed on his pipe.

'I reckon that the best bet is to drive them

steers into the pass as fast as they can run. Stampede the brutes.'

Johnny turned his head and looked into the smiling face.

'That's a darn loco idea, Cookie.'

'Yep. But you thought of it first.'

The young trail boss moved to the pinto pony and untied his reins. His eyes glanced heavenward and his gloved hand gripped the saddle horn before he poked the toe of his left boot into the leather stirrup. He mounted the pony slowly. There was still at least an hour or more before dawn, he thought.

Johnny Puma looked around the area. He concentrated on the huge herd of longhorn steers a quarter of a mile away from the chuck wagon and the camp-fire. The cattle were still on their bellies and that was the way Johnny wanted them to stay until the sun emerged from over the horizon.

There were no more dangerous animals on the face of the earth than the famed Texan longhorns when they stampeded and

Johnny knew that the easiest way to get the massive beasts skittish was to try and move them during the darkness of night.

Only the heat of the day could slow the herd down enough for his cowboys to have any chance of controlling them.

'You figuring on getting them steers on their feet, Johnny?' Cookie asked.

'Nope. I intend keeping them on the ground as long as possible,' the trail boss replied. 'I'll wait until sun-up before I order the boys to get them steers rolling.' Cookie began to gather up the tin plates that the cowboys had hurriedly discarded after their early breakfast. He gripped the pipe between his teeth and stared up at the troubled rider.

'I'll pack the wagon up and be ready to follow you guys into the pass. You just give me the signal and I'll whip my team of horses into action faster than you can spit.'

Johnny teased his mount forward and then leaned on the saddle horn and looked down at the face he had known since he had first arrived on the Bar 10.

'No, Cookie. You turn this chuck wagon around and head back home when I get those steers running.'

The face of the older man looked confused. 'But I'm ready to follow you and the rest of the crew. Them dry-gulchers don't worry me none. Where you and the boys go, I intend following, Johnny.'

Johnny Puma said nothing for a few moments. Then he nodded, turned the pinto around and rode towards the herd. Men like old Cookie were impossible to argue with.

They had been around too long to fear anything.

Even logic.

The Bar 10 seemed to breed men of grit, and Cookie was no exception.

Cookie was as much a part of the Bar 10 as any of the cowboys and wranglers who rode under Gene Adams's brand. He had proved his bravery countless times and had never turned his back on danger. Cookie kicked dust over the embers of the fire and knew that when Johnny gave the signal, he would be driving his chuck wagon into the pass with his trusty Colt at his side.

The pinto pony slowed and began to circle the herd with the rest of the crew. Even in the moonlight Johnny could see the anxious faces of his men aimed in his direction. He allowed the pony to catch up with Happy Summers before reining in.

Neither man spoke.

Now Johnny had to tell each of the cowboys what he wanted them to do.

It was not going to be easy.

It would be his toughest test yet.

NINE

Gene Adams spurred the chestnut mare on and drove alongside his friend Tomahawk as they continued heading towards the distant ridge. They had made excellent time as they travelled across the cruel merciless desert towards the outcrop of massive rocks that they knew would lead them to the fresh running water that wound its way through the maze of canyons within Deadman's Fork.

For nearly an hour they had been pushing their mounts harder than either of them liked. Their horses were exhausted and normally the pair of Bar 10 riders would have taken the heavy saddles from their backs and rested them for hours.

But this was not a land to dwell in for even a second longer than necessary.

Death lurked here waiting for them to make a mistake.

Both determined riders knew that they had to get out of this desert and reach Deadman's Fork as soon as possible. For that was the only place where it was possible to fill their dry canteens and allow their horses to drink their fill.

Both horses had been forced far beyond their limits and yet faithfully continued trying to obey their masters.

Adams stood high in his stirrups and leaned as far forward as he dared in order to take the weight off the back of the chestnut mare. But he continued forcing the animal to gallop when he knew that the horse was ready to drop.

It was a calculated risk, but one Adams was willing to take. He had lived his life taking such risks. That was why he had survived when so many of his contemporaries had not.

'How much further, Tomahawk?' Adams called across to the rider on the smaller mount.

'Another half-mile, I reckon,' Tomahawk called back as he held on to his reins and tried to urge the black gelding to find yet another turn of speed.

Gene Adams could see the wall of giant boulders rapidly looming up before them and knew that they would soon have to turn their horses and ride for at least another mile or so before they reached the pass that would give them access into Deadman's Fork.

As the land beneath the hoofs of their spent mounts changed from the arid desert terrain to the soft beginning of the huge range, the two men began to haul their reins to the left.

The smaller horse seemed to take the change of direction in its stride but the taller chestnut began to stumble as it vainly tried to cope with the markedly different going.

Tomahawk pulled his horse up as his tired eyes noted that his friend was in trouble.

Suddenly, without warning the tall mare crashed heavily to the ground.

Adams had been trying to steady his mount for more than a furlong when he felt the long-legged staggering on the slippery grass that spread out from the ridge wall.

Yet when he felt the chestnut buckling beneath his saddle, it came as a total surprise to the experienced horseman. In the blinking of an eye, the rancher found himself being hurtled helplessly through the air.

Gene Adams had been bucked off many a horse in his day but never like this. Instinctively, he had raised his gloved hands before hitting the unyielding surface, but he rolled fast and hard into the solid boulders at the foot of the ridge.

Tomahawk turned his horse around quickly and leapt to the ground. Like a man half his age, he ran to the side of the prostrate rancher.

'You OK, Gene?' the old-timer asked feverishly. He knelt down by the side of the motionless figure. 'Answer me, darn it.'

There was no response.

Tomahawk's bony hands reached around the rancher's shoulders and carefully turned him over. Blood covered the face of the unconscious Adams.

It was a sight that chilled Tomahawk.

'Talk to me, Gene,' he pleaded, trying to wipe the blood away from the face he could no longer recognize. 'Wake up, ya young fool. What the heck am I meant to do if'n you don't tell me? Come on, son. Open them eyes.'

Tomahawk carefully eased Adams's head down on to the grass and tried to think of what he ought to do if he were to help his oldest pal. His mind raced.

Water! That was it. Water!

He stood up and snapped his fingers.

Tomahawk knew that he had better head on into the pass and get the water that he and Gene had been heading for. But he would have to bring it back here and try and revive the rancher.

The old-timer ran across to his lathered-up horse and mounted the creature. He did not want to leave his friend lying alone at the foot of the towering ridge but knew he had no choice.

As he dragged his reins hard to his right he saw the chestnut mare clambering to its feet. The animal was winded but seemed to be in better shape than its master.

Tomahawk spurred the black gelding and galloped off in the direction of the pass.

TEN

US Marshal Cody Cannon had been in McCoy since his golden half-hunter pocket-watch had chimed three times in his vest pocket, when the massive locomotive rolled to a stop alongside the hundreds of cattle pens. He had spent more than an hour making sure that his prized appaloosa stallion had been taken from the flatbed carriage at the rear of the long train, and led to the livery stables with all his trail gear and tack. For Cody Cannon was a man who never rented saddle horses: he always rode his own well-trained mount. He had learned long ago that in the West, a faithful horse was a man's most valuable asset.

As was his way, he had arrived un-announced and unnoticed by those he was paid to protect and keep under control. For more than six months the sturdy, well-built man had been trying to get the authority to venture into the notorious cattle town and its surrounding district. For he had noticed, when all others had not, that far too many herds of Texan cattle had been disappearing on their way to McCoy.

Cannon bore little resemblance to the usual men who wore a star and enforced the law. He looked far older than he actually was and had little height, but he was a match for any of his more flamboyant counterparts.

Cody Cannon had brains and an expertise with his handguns and rifle which had kept him alive far longer than men of his dangerous occupation could usually boast. His name had become known in towns that he had yet to visit but few people had any knowledge of what the marshal even looked like.

Cannon stepped out of the shadows of the less than fragrant railhead area and made his way up into the sprawling town which he had never before had the call to investigate.

He began to sense the dangers that this place held for the innocent and unwary.

McCoy was a town where dozens of narrow alleys linked wider streets. Each alley held the possibility for the ruthless to kill those who ventured into their unlit lengths.

Cannon pulled his large hat down over his forehead and stared ahead. He carried his saddlebags over one shoulder and rested the palm of his right hand on the grip of one of his deadly Colt Peacemakers.

The moon was big and bright but its light seemed unable to penetrate into the shadows that filled the alleys and twisting corners that made up the best part of the cattle town. Yet there were no shadows that could frighten Cody Cannon.

He walked with short steps that allowed him always to be balanced for action.

If anyone came out of the blackness, either to try and rob or to kill him, they would taste the accuracy of his famed guns. He feared no one.

Cannon paused at the rear of a line of

wood-and-brick-built structures and studied the area carefully with his hooded eyes. He knew that somewhere within this town he would find the answer as to who was ambushing so many of the herds that had been trying to get to McCoy's famous auction houses.

McCoy held the answer.

It was the only town within a hundred square miles and if it were not for the railtracks that had been laid down to allow thousands of steers a month to be transported back East, it would have been yet another ghost town by now.

The wealth of this town depended totally on the railhead it fostered. There was money here, Cannon could smell it as easily as he could the stench that drifted up from the stock-pens behind him.

Men had become wealthy in McCoy.

Most had done it legally but others had simply used their strength, greed and deadly guns to acquire it from its rightful owners.

Cody Cannon spat at the ground and then

placed a cigar between his teeth and lit it. He could hear the sound of people enjoying themselves coming from all directions and knew that places like McCoy never actually stopped supplying pleasures to its customers as long as they had the money to pay for it. Whether it was hard liquor, gambling or simply female company, it was all available at a price to the cowboys who had just been paid off after a long trail drive.

The marshal continued walking.

Unlike lesser more fearful men, he chose not to take the safest route, which was well illuminated, but rather the maze of alleys that stretched out before him. Either would lead him to his destination: the sheriff's office on the main street, but the alleys would ensure that he got there unseen.

Cannon had walked steadily for several minutes when he noticed the crumpled body lying amid the filth that always filled the alleys of such towns.

The marshal knelt down and studied the body of Hec Smith before he hauled it up from the ground with powerful hands and arms and draped it over his right shoulder.

The lifeless Smith weighed little and hardly slowed the pace of the lawman as he walked out into the long main street. Again he paused and surveyed the scene.

It was still busy.

He stared up and down the length of the street at the men who wandered in various states of drunkenness from one saloon to the next. Then he spotted the faded painted sign he had been seeking. The word SHERIFF seemed to draw him like a moth to a naked flame.

Sucking on the cigar, Cannon marched across the street through the moonlight and the yellow glow that spread out from the street-lanterns and storefronts until he reached the office.

The marshal stepped up on to the board-walk and looked at the locked door of the office, which was bathed in darkness. He kicked at the door like an angry mountain goat until he saw a man appearing from the back room, carrying a candle in one hand and a cocked pistol in the other.

'Who is it?' Sheriff Dick Hayes shouted at the figure with the body on his shoulder that his sleep-filled eyes could see.

'Marshal Cody Cannon. Open this damn door.'

Hayes turned the key in the lock and was knocked backwards by the burly man as he marched into the office and dropped the body on to the cluttered desk.

'That's Hec, the telegraph-office man,' Hayes gasped, holding the candle over the face of the corpse.

Cannon sucked in a lungful of smoke and flicked the ash from the end of his cigar.

'He's been stabbed with a long stiletto, Sheriff.'

'Who would do such a thing?' Hayes gasped.

'Get some clothes on and we'll try and find out,' Cannon said, dropping his saddle-bags on the chair behind the desk.

'But how, Cannon?'

Cody Cannon stared hard at the man. 'Stick with me and I'll teach you how to be a real lawman.'

Hayes looked hard at the stone-faced marshal. 'What's that meant to imply?'

'Ain't you heard of clues?' Cannon asked. 'When you get some clothes on we'll go to the telegraph office and try and find out what his last message was.'

'What? Why?' Hayes did not know where to start.

'Because I got me an idea that the last message he took down will lead us to his killer.'

'That don't make no sense.'

'It will.' Cannon inhaled on the cigar again. 'I promise you, it will.'

The two lawmen reached the locked telegraph office and looked in through the glass panel of the door. A still-glowing oil-lamp rested on the desk next to the notepads and telegraph equipment.

'Looks like Hec Smith left in a hurry,

Cannon,' Hayes said, watching the marshal remove a fine metal rod from the inside pocket of his jacket.

'Yep. He left his post to give someone the message he had received, Sheriff,' Cannon said. He slipped the metal rod into the lock and twisted it.

The sound of the lock tumbler's clicking filled both men's ears. The marshal smiled and then opened the door.

'How'd you do that?' Hayes asked, following Cannon in to the telegraph office and up to the desk.

Cannon slipped the fine rod back into his jacket pocket and sat down at the desk. He picked up the blank notepad and held it beneath the oil-lamp's glass globe.

'Good. We're lucky,' he said.

Hayes scratched his chin. 'We are? How?'

'Smith was a heavy-handed writer,' Cannon replied. He focused on the impressions left on the sheet of paper in his hand. 'I can read the message he wrote out. The impression is still on the sheet below the one he must have taken to whoever it was needed the information.'

Hayes watched as the marshal carefully rubbed a pencil across the paper until the impressed dots and dashes became clear.

'But that's in telegraph lingo, Cannon. How is that gonna do us any good?'

Cody Cannon held the paper under the lamp again and started to read it aloud.

'It's to the head auctioneer from a Gene Adams of the Bar 10 ranch. It says that he's sending a herd of his prime longhorns to McCoy and a certain Johnny Puma is in control of the cattle drive.'

Hayes rubbed his chin again. 'I ought to have figured that you could read that nonsense.'

'This confirms my suspicions, Sheriff,' answered Cody Cannon. He rose to his feet and put the scrap of paper in his pocket. 'I knew that someone at this office had to be selling information about approaching cattle drives to whoever it is behind the ambushes. This proves that Hec Smith was involved and he got himself killed because he probably got a tad greedy.'

Sheriff Hayes raised both eyebrows and followed the marshal out into the street.

'Hec was in with the rustlers?'

'Yep.' Cannon stared at the array of busy buildings that faced them and wondered which of them held the man who was behind the series of attacks on the cattle drives. He focused on the impressive Diamond Garter Gaming House. 'Who owns that gambling hall, Sheriff?'

'Madison Barton, Cannon. Why?'

'Because I found Smith's body in the alley next to it.'

'We paying Barton a visit?' Hayes asked.

Cannon shook his head. 'Not yet. First we have to go to the head auctioneer and find out whether Smith delivered the message. If he didn't, then we'll go and have us a chat with Madison Barton.'

The sheriff pointed down the street. 'The auctioneer lives down here a piece. But he'll be asleep now.'

Marshal Cannon walked next to the sheriff. 'Then we'll wake him up. I have to act fast.'

'What's the hurry?'

'By my reckoning the Bar 10 herd must be darn close to McCoy by now and that means innocent men will die if we don't do something.'

The pair of law officers continued walking down the long street in the direction of the houses which lay at the very edge of the cattle town.

ELEVEN

Dust rose off the black gelding's hoofs into the moonlit air as an anxious Tomahawk thundered along at the foot of the high wall of boulders atop his exhausted mount. He was like a man possessed as his hands slapped reins from one side of his horse's shoulders to the other.

There was but a single thought in his mind: to reach the crystal-clear water which he knew flowed through the maze of canyons deep within the heart of Deadman's Fork. He had to get water back to his friend at all costs.

The ancient cowboy steered the black gelding towards the mouth of the pass and galloped straight in between the high sides of the gigantic boulders. The sound of his horse's hoofs echoed off the canyon walls as he drove straight towards the place where he knew he could fill his canteen.

More than a score of rifles were trained on him as he forced the quarter horse across the dust, but Tomahawk had no idea that his back had become a target for so many cocked and readied Winchesters.

On the highest point of the crags, Sam Flint raised his arms to his men and signalled for them not to open fire on the solitary horseman. He knew that Johnny Puma and the 500 longhorns were too close for any of his own men to open fire. They dare not open up with their guns before the longhorns were all making their way through the twisting pass below them.

A single shot now could warn the Bar 10 riders and stop them driving the cattle into the canyon pass.

Flint made his way down from the top of the rock-face, clutching his razor-sharp knife in his hand. He moved past one of his henchmen after another until he spotted the figure twenty feet below him.

Tomahawk had dismounted and was kneeling beside the shallow, fast-flowing water which cut through the canyons.

Bodine Bonny had trailed Sam Flint to the spot above the unsuspecting cowboy.

'Who is that?' Bonny asked.

'I ain't sure, but whoever he is he'll not see fifty again,' Flint replied. His hand toyed with the lethal stiletto as his anxious mind considered leaping down and silently stabbing the aged intruder.

'He looks kinda ragged, like a mountain

man,' Bonny said, clutching his rifle across his chest. 'He's no threat to us by the looks of it. He's only here collecting water.'

Flint screwed up his eyes and stared down at the crouching figure. There was something about the man that he thought he recognized, and it troubled him.

'I'm sure that I've seen that critter before,' he said quietly.

'Maybe he's one of the gold-miners from over in the territory, Sam,' Bonny suggested. 'They all look like that. Whiskers and skinny. That must be where you seen him.'

'I ain't so sure.' Sam Flint moved further along the ledge that he and the larger man were standing upon. He then knelt and tried to get an even better view of their unexpected visitor.

'Quit worrying, Sam. He'll probably hightail it out of here as fast as he rode in once he has his water. There ain't no way he can interfere with our plans.'

Flint knew that he had seen the man before and was not convinced it had been in the goldfields as Bodine Bonny had suggested.

'He might be from the herd. He might be one of the Bar 10 men, Bodine.'

Bonny sighed. 'An old relic like that?'

Suddenly Sam Flint stood up and looked straight into his companion's eyes.

'That's one of Gene Adams's men. I recall seeing him in McCoy a couple of years back when the Bar 10 brought in a massive herd of longhorns,' Flint recalled. 'He's one of Adams's best pals and is named Tomahawk, account of he carries an old Indian hatchet.'

Bodine Bonny shrugged. 'Even so, he ain't spotted us. You ain't intending sticking him with ya knife, I hope?'

Sam Flint looked at the deadly weapon gripped in his hand, then his eyes flashed down at Tomahawk who was now hanging the full canteen on his saddle horn. He knew that if he were to try and kill the bearded old-timer, he would have to do it fast and silently. The odds were against his being able to achieve either task.

'We'll let him go,' Flint said signalling the

other bushwhackers not to do anything. 'There's no way that I can get down there fast enough to stick him before he lets a shot off with his Colt.'

Bonny nodded and both he and Flint watched the elderly cowboy mounting up and spurring the black gelding hard. The eyes of thirty men followed Tomahawk until he had ridden out of the pass and was headed towards the moonlit range.

'I don't get it, Sam,' Bonny said as the two men made their way back to their high vantage points amid the massive boulders.

'What?'

'That old man's horse was lathered up real bad.'

'So?'

'So why didn't he let the horse drink its fill and rest before he lit out?' Bonny was curious.

Flint stopped in his tracks and pondered the question.

'That's right, Bodine. That Tomahawk varmint rode in here like his life depended

98

on him reaching the water and then he rode out just as fast. Why?'

Bonny rested himself once more against the smooth boulder which had supported him for so many hours.

'I bet that he was collecting water for someone.'

Flint rubbed his chin. 'Someone who must be hurt bad.'

'You say that this old Tomahawk character is Gene Adams's best pal?' Bonny gave a fleeting glance at Flint before he pointed down at the range which was still bathed in the bluish light of the large moon. The dust from Tomahawk's horse was still lingering, showing the exact route the rider had taken. 'If he's a Bar 10 man, then how come he didn't head back to the herd? How come he rode thataway toward the desert?'

Sam Flint had no answers.

Only curiosity.

'Get my horse. I'm gonna trail that old varmint.'

TWELVE

Larry Drake had been circling the longhorns for nearly two hours when Johnny Puma rode up to him. The experienced wrangler was the last of the Bar 10 cowboys whom Johnny had to inform about his daredevil plan of stampeding the mighty herd into the pass.

The two riders drew their mounts close and Larry leant across to grip the saddle horn of his friend's pinto pony.

'What's wrong, Johnny?'

The young trail boss gazed into Larry's face and then lowcred his head. He was dog-tired, both physically and mentally. There was a desperation in the rider that he might make a mistake which would cost the lives of those who trusted his judgement.

Johnny tilted his head. 'I've told the rest of

the boys that when the sun rises, we gotta get the herd on its feet and then stampede them, Larry.'

The wrangler bit his dry lip. He could hardly believe the words that had just come from the mouth of the young trail boss.

'Are you serious, Johnny?'

Johnny looked up again. 'Dead serious, partner. We have to try and get these long-horns running and then force the critters into the pass. We have to spook them so that they won't stop running until they reach McCoy.'

'But why?' Larry asked in disbelief.

'There are dry-gulchers up in the crags to both sides of the pass, Larry,' Johnny explained. 'I figure the only chance we've got is to frighten these steers and drive them hard.'

Larry Drake released his grip on his friend's saddle and gazed through the moonlight at the wall of massive boulders a mile or so north of the sleeping herd. He knew that it was a perfect place for an ambush.

'We could take a few of the boys and try and shoot it out with them horn toads, Johnny.'

'The moon is too big. They'd pick us off as soon as we got within range of their rifles. Besides, the sound of gunfire would only cause the steers to spook and there would be no way that we could control them then.'

Larry tried to think.

'But to try and get these steers all fired up is dangerous and might cost us some lives too.' Larry rubbed his mouth on the back of one of his gloves. 'What happens if we do manage to get the steers to enter the pass? If there are men up in the crags, won't they still start shooting at us when we chase the herd into it?'

'Five hundred head can make an awful lot of dust, Larry,' Johnny said. 'I'm hoping it'll make enough dust to make it impossible for them riflemen to spot us.'

'Enough dust to give us cover? That's a mighty big gamble, Johnny.' Larry sighed nervously. 'The ground still has dew on it and that ain't the best recipe for making dust. Are you sure that this is our only option?'

'I'll be honest with you.' Johnny exhaled. 'I ain't sure of anything any more, Larry. I wish that Gene was here to make all the decisions, but he ain't. That means I have to try and work things out myself. I tell you something for nothing, pal. It ain't easy.'

'Whatever you decide, I'll follow you, Johnny.' Larry smiled at his friend. 'You just give the order and I'll obey it.'

Before he could respond, Johnny caught a glimpse of something out of the corner of his eye. He pulled his reins back, turned the pinto and stared at the wall of towering rocks. He squinted hard and then pointed.

'Do you see that dust, Larry? There, close to the rocks. A rider heading east.'

'Yep. I see him,' Larry answered. He stood in his stirrups and stared long and hard at the distant rider.

'Look, another one,' Johnny said as the sun began to creep out of the distant horizon sending shafts of light skimming across the open range. 'See him? He's trailing the first one.'

'What you gonna do?' Larry asked his excited pal.

'I just want to find out who that is who's heading towards the desert in such a damn hurry, Larry,' Johnny said, holding his mount in check.

'But what about the herd? The stampede and all?'

Johnny gathered up his reins and turned he pony hard to his left.

'I'm gonna go take me a look-see. Don't do nothing until I get back, Larry.'

Johnny swung the pinto around and jabbed his spurs into its flesh. The young Bar 10 rider drove the handsome mount hard in the direction of the distant dust. He had no idea who it was riding across the face of the ridge, but he intended to find out.

THIRTEEN

Tomahawk reined in, scrambled from his saddle and ran across the ground to his prostrate friend. His bony fingers unscrewed the stopper of the canteen as he dropped on to his knees at Gene Adams's side. The unconscious rancher had not moved a muscle in all the time that Tomahawk had been away. He looked more dead than alive.

The old-timer gently pushed the palm of his left hand beneath the nape of Adams's neck and carefully lifted his head. He put the open neck of the canteen to Adams's lips and poured some of the ice-cold water into his open mouth.

At first the water just trickled from the corner of Gene Adams's mouth, but slowly it seemed to be having an effect as the rancher began to swallow.

'You OK, Gene?' Tomahawk asked.

The rancher still did not reply.

Tomahawk raised the canteen and poured the precious liquid over the bloodstained temples of his friend until the silver hair was soaked. Adams moved his head back and forth as the cold water began to revive him.

'Wake up, Gene. C'mon now. Wake up,' Tomahawk implored the stunned man.

Slowly Gene's eyelids flickered until they managed to open. At first his eyes seemed to be staring blankly at the sky as dawn at last arrived and colour crept stealthily across the heavens.

'You awake now, boy?' Tomahawk asked.

Adams blinked hard a few times and looked at Tomahawk.

'What happened?'

'You took a tumble, Gene.'

'How's my horse?'

'She's OK.'

Gene Adams managed to pull himself up until he was sitting beside the kneeling Tomahawk. His gloved fingers tugged at the jutting beard.

'I must be getting old. There was a time when I would have just bounced off the ground and got back up if my horse threw me.'

Tomahawk chuckled.

'You bounced sure enough. A couple of times.'

Suddenly both men were aware of the sound of hoofs behind them. They turned and looked hard at the rider who had been following Tomahawk, now dragging his mount to a halt a dozen feet behind them.

After chewing on the dust that drifted from the hoofs of the rider's mount, the Bar 10 men spotted the Winchester that was trained on them.

Sam Flint smiled as he stared down the length of his rifle at the two men on the ground before him.

'Now, if I ain't mistaken, I think that I must be in the company of the famed Gene Adams and his trusty sidekick, Tomahawk,' Flint drawled.

Adams rubbed his hand across his mouth and studied the rider.

'You have the advantage of me, stranger.'

'Damn right!' Flint spat. 'And I ain't gonna waste that advantage either.'

Tomahawk felt the handle of his trusty hatchet in his hand.

'If'n ya knows who we are, how come you got a rifle aimed at us, mister?'

Flint did not reply. He turned in the saddle and aimed his rifle at the approaching Johnny Puma. He squeezed the trigger. All three men saw the Stetson being torn from Johnny's head before the young rider reined in and stopped his horse.

Flint laughed, pushing the Winchester lever down and back up again until the rifle magazine was once more primed for action.

'That was a good shot, stranger,' Adams said.

'Not really. I was aiming at his belly.' Flint shrugged. He moved his horse a little closer to the pair of men on the ground.

'What you want of us?' Tomahawk snorted.

'I want that herd,' Flint replied.

'There ain't no way that you'll get them steers!' Tomahawk said as he got to his feet.

Sam Flint stared into the eyes of the defiant old man.

'Get on your horse and ride to Johnny Puma. Tell him that he will escort the long-horns into the pass and then take his entire crew back to the Bar 10.'

Tomahawk looked down at Gene Adams in total shock, then returned his attention to the rider.

'You can't make me do anything, mister. I ain't afraid of ya.'

Flint nodded.

'If you don't, I will kill Gene Adams and then I shall kill you.'

Adams cleared his throat and tugged at the pants leg of his oldest friend until he had his attention.

'Do as he says, Tomahawk. I don't think he's bluffing.'

FOURTEEN

Madison Barton had defied the odds for his entire life. He had no intention of stopping now. It was said that a card-sharp never wore rings, for they hampered his ability to use sleight of hand when manipulating a pack of cards. But Barton's hands were covered in golden rings of all sizes and designs and his fingers could still divert any onlooker from noticing when he had palmed a vital ace or any other desired card that would enable him to win a poker-game.

He had noticed the sunlight outside the window as he dealt yet another game of five-card stud to the two men who had somehow survived the long night at his private table. Barton had allowed the two men who still faced him to win several hands because it was good politics, when faced with the town mayor and the owner of the largest bank in McCoy, to offer a few crumbs of hope before finishing them off.

Barton knew that they would think that they had come close to defeating the professional gambler and that would bring them back again.

There was another reason for keeping the two wealthy men engrossed in the game. For they would be his alibi, should anyone ever think that he was involved with the rustlers whom he controlled.

Madison Barton knew that there would be no one within the boundaries of McCoy who would doubt the words of these two town stalwarts. If they said Barton was playing poker with them all night, then that was what he was doing.

But Barton had not taken into account the dogged determination of the US Marshal who was on his scent. For Cody Cannon had started to piece together a case that even the wily gambler would find it hard to talk himself out of.

For unlike most lawmen who roamed the West, Cannon had a brain that was calculating and precise. He looked for and found clues where others would never have even thought that they existed.

Madison Barton had no idea that a net was being closed around him by the one man who was capable of catching him.

Cannon had his prey cornered.

All the clues led to the Diamond Garter Gaming House. And Marshal Cody Cannon knew it. All he had to do was use those clues and nail the guilty party down. Cannon led the still-confused Sheriff Dick Hayes along the long street with the search warrant in his hand.

'Judge Cooper sure was mad when we woke him up, Cannon,' Hayes said as the two men turned the corner, mounted the boardwalk and started along the main street in the direction of the gambling-house.

'You have to do things legal if you want to ruffle a few feathers, Sheriff,' Cannon said.

'But what did we need a search warrant for?' Hayes asked as he tried to keep pace with the determined marshal. 'What is it that we're gonna search for?'

Cannon paused at the edge of the boardwalk opposite the Diamond Garter. He pushed the warrant into his pocket and then pushed his coat tails over the grips of his guns.

'I just want to frighten Madison Barton enough for him to do something,' the marshal said.

'I don't understand none of this.'

'Just stick close and cover my back,' Cannon ordered. 'I don't think he's the sort who would back-shoot a lawman, but you never know.'

'But Madison Barton is one of the most respectable men in McCoy,' Hayes protested. 'I reckon that he must also be one of the richest.'

Cody Cannon raised an eyebrow. 'We have to find out how come he's one of the richest, Sheriff. By what I've heard of this dude, he ain't earned all that money by playing cards.'

Hayes stooped to address the shorter man. 'He couldn't have nothing to do with the cattle rustling, Cannon. I never even seen him ride a horse.'

Cannon shook his head. 'I have a theory that whoever is rustling those herds is taking orders from someone like Barton. Someone who has a good name and prominent position in McCoy. A man whom nobody would suspect.'

'But how ya gonna prove that?'

'Clues, my friend. Clues.' Cannon stepped down on to the sandy ground and headed in to the alley where he had discovered the body of Hec Smith only a few hours earlier. The sheriff trailed the stocky man. 'We have to prove a link. Or we have to make Barton believe that we've got proof of a link.'

'What if he's innocent, Cannon?' Hayes asked.

The marshal stopped and studied the blood-soaked wall where he had found

Smith. He knelt down, brushed the litter aside with his right hand and studied the area carefully.

'If Madison Barton is innocent, he has nothing to fear from me, Hayes.'

The sheriff was about to speak again when he heard a satisfied sound coming from Cannon's mouth. Hayes pushed his hat back from his forehead and watched in amazement as the marshal rose to his feet, holding something in his hand.

'What is that you've got there, Cannon?'

Cody Cannon carefully folded whatever it was he had found and pulled out a brown paper bag from the deep hip-pocket. He dropped the object into the bag and then placed the bag back into the pocket.

'What was that?' Hayes repeated his question.

Cannon raised his head and smiled. 'The rope that might just hang our gambling friend, Sheriff.'

FIFTEEN

It was a frantic Larry Drake who drove his horse across the sun-baked range towards the two familiar horsemen. Reaching them, he hauled in his reins and circled Tomahawk and Johnny Puma before stopping his skittish mount.

'Them steers are on the rise, Johnny. That damn shot spooked them good. I don't think that me and the boys can keep them contained.'

Johnny said nothing. His eyes and every ounce of his concentration was on the distant rifleman and Gene Adams bathed in sunlight in front of the massive rockface. He still did not understand what either of his friends were doing here, when they ought to have been back at the Bar 10.

But they were here. One was at his side

and the other had a rifle aimed at him.

'Did ya hear me, Johnny?' Larry shouted at the younger man. He turned his horse and stared back at the groaning longhorn steers who were rising angrily to their feet. 'Them steers gonna stampede of their own account unless we do something fast.'

Tomahawk moved his black quarter horse close to the frightened wrangler and pointed at the herd.

'Get them cowboys out of there, Larry. Move them to the chuck wagon. These longhorns are gonna start running in all directions and them cowboys are gonna get themselves trampled if they don't get behind them.'

Larry Drake's face suddenly changed expression. 'What are you doin' here, Tomahawk?'

Tomahawk slapped his hat across the rear of Larry's mount and then pointed again. 'Just do what I told ya.'

The wrangler galloped back towards the rest of the Bar 10 cowboys. There was not a second to lose. The longhorns had been awoken by the rifle shot that had taken Johnny's Stetson off his head and they were angry.

Johnny pulled on his reins and made his horse back up until he was above his hat. He held on to his saddle horn and then scooped the hat off the ground and stared at it. He pushed his finger through one of the bullet holes in it and then glanced at Tomahawk.

'That was close. That varmint almost hit me.'

Tomahawk stood in his stirrups, reached across and ran a finger across Johnny's brow. He showed it to the stunned youngster.

It was covered in blood.

'He didn't miss ya, Johnny,' Tomahawk said.

Johnny looked angry and touched the top of his scalp. He flinched and then screwed up his eyes as he focused on the distant men. One he thought of as a father and the other someone he did not know, but wanted to real bad.

'Who is that varmint, Tomahawk?' Johnny snapped as his eyes flashed from the herd behind them to the men before them. 'What's going on here?'

'I ain't sure. He just come out of nowhere and told us that he wants our herd,' Tomahawk answered honestly.

Johnny's head turned. He looked hard into the wrinkled old face. A face that he trusted.

'He must be one of the dry-gulchers who are hid up in the crags, old-timer. There's a whole bunch of the critters lying in wait for us.'

Tomahawk raised his bushy eyebrows. 'What dry-gulchers?'

Johnny pointed, then carefully placed his hat back on head. 'The dry-gulchers who are covering both sides of the canyon walls overlooking the pass.'

Tomahawk swallowed hard. He suddenly realized how close he must have come to getting himself shot when he rode into the pass to fill his canteen.

'Gosh. I never seen them back-shooters

when I rode in and out of there.'

'They seen you OK. That's why one of them trailed ya back to Gene.'

Tomahawk touched the sleeve of his pal. Even with his poor long-range eyesight, he could see that the cowboys were losing their battle with the longhorns.

'That *hombre* wants the herd, but I reckon that the herd has plans of its own. Look at 'em, Johnny. Look.'

Johnny spun his pinto pony full circle and stared at the phalanx of snorting longhorns. They were getting angrier by the heartbeat and he suddenly felt very afraid.

'What we gonna do, Tomahawk?'

'First we better get back to the chuck wagon, Johnny,' the old-timer said. 'We don't stand a chance if them steers head this way.'

'But how are we gonna help Gene, Tomahawk?'

The old cowboy rubbed his whiskers and tried to reply. He had no answers.

SIXTEEN

Madison Barton's eyes flashed upward from the five cards that he held in his left hand as the fingers of his right toyed with the stack of gaming-chips. He suddenly felt that even a full house might not be enough to win this particular hand.

The sight of the unfamiliar figure moving from the ornate doorway, with Sheriff Dick Hayes a few steps behind him, made Barton take notice.

The gleaming star on Cody Cannon's vest made it clear what this intruder was. Barton sat upright and watched as the lawman brushed the two well-built doormen aside as if they were nothing more than window drapes.

The sturdy marshal stopped at the table and stared at the trio of card-players. It did not take more than a second for him to work out which of them was Barton.

'I got me a warrant to search these premises, Barton,' Cannon said, tossing the paper on to the stack of gaming-chips. 'I intend exercising that warrant.'

The owner of the gaming-hall placed his cards down on the green baize and smiled at the mayor and banker.

'I think that the pot is yours, gentlemen,' Barton said, rising to his feet.

'Who is this man, Barton?' a flustered mayor asked.

'What seems to be the trouble?' the banker added.

Cannon pulled the lapel of his heavy jacket just far enough away from his bandanna for both of Barton's gambling opponents to see the tin star pinned to his vest.

'I'd like to see your office, Barton,' Cannon growled.

Barton looked at Hayes. 'What's going on here, Sheriff?'

Dick Hayes shrugged. 'I ain't got the

foggiest, Mr Barton. But Marshal Cannon knows his business.'

'My apologies, gentlemen.' Barton nodded at the two men seated at the table and then led Cannon and Hayes towards the rear of the building, where his office was situated. 'Follow me, Marshal. I have no idea what this about but I'm willing to humour you.'

Cannon trailed the elegant man through the highly decorated gambling-house and into the private office. Sheriff Hayes remained in the open doorframe and watched the two other men as they moved around the office.

Barton was nervous and sat on the edge of his large desk. He could not take his eyes off the strange figure who seemed determined to find something to implicate the gambling-house owner.

To Hayes, it was like watching an old hound-dog seeking out a possum trail. The sheriff could not take his eyes off the silent lawman as he moved methodically around the exquisite office. But Cannon did not see either the expensive paintings or the priceless ornaments which lavishly decorated every inch of the room.

All Cannon could see were the signs that a man had brutally met his Maker in this place. The clues were all there for someone as sharp-witted as Cannon to find.

Sweat began to trace its way down Barton's temples. He was filled with awe and fear by the strange man who was walking around his office, looking at the floor until he found what he was seeking.

Faster than a man of his build should have been capable of, the marshal knelt and ran his hand over the highly polished floorboards.

'What is it, Cannon?' Hayes asked curiously.

The marshal looked up at the sheriff. 'A few spots of what looks like blood, Hayes.'

Madison Barton cleared his throat and then moved from the edge of the desk until he was standing behind it, near the window.

'I'd like to see you prove that what you've found there is actually blood, Marshal. For all any of us know, those spots are simply spittle from one of my employees who happens to like chewing tobacco,' Barton said.

Cannon rose and did not respond to the gambler. He turned and walked across the room until he was looking at the door that led to the alley.

'I don't think that this is spittle, Barton.'

Barton felt a cold chill running up his spine as he focused on the dried bloodstains which covered and surrounded the door-handle. Bloodstains that had been left by Sam Flint when he carried the body of Hec Smith from the office and dumped him in the alley.

'This is a bloody handprint, Barton,' Cannon announced.

'I don't understand, sir. What is all this talk about blood stains, anyway?' Barton bluffed as only a professional gambler could or would.

Cannon moved slowly towards the desk and the man who stood tall behind it.

'Hec Smith was killed in this room sometime last night, Barton. Whether you did it or you got one of your flunkies to do it, I don't know. The fact remains that this is where he died. In your private office.'

'There is no way that you could prove that to a jury, Marshal,' Barton said, lowering his head. 'I'm a highly respectable man in McCoy and I doubt very much whether you could convince anyone that I've done anything wrong.'

Cannon reached into his jacket's deep pocket and produced the paper bag. He carefully opened it and reached inside.

Madison Barton's eyes were trained on the bag as Cannon's fingers withdrew the object he had found amid the blood and filth in the alley.

'Recognize this, Barton?' Cody Cannon held the portion of headed notepaper out to the saloon-owner, who was sweating. It was covered in bloody fingerprints. 'It's your headed notepaper.'

'I don't understand.' The gambler watched as Cannon stepped up to the opposite side of the desk. He was standing in exactly the same spot where Hec Smith had stood before Sam Flint's lethal stiletto had been thrust straight through his thin body.

Cannon looked down at the desk.

'I figure, by the blood on the floor and the ones on your papers, that Smith must have been standing exactly on this spot.'

Madison Barton looked down in horror at his pile of usually neat papers. Of the top sheet only part remained. It was, indeed, covered in spots of blood.

Cannon carefully placed the segment of paper he had found earlier beside the top sheet. They fitted together. It was a perfect match.

'Smith was knifed here. The long blade went straight through his pitifully lean body and blood was splattered over your desk, but you didn't notice, did you? In the throes of death, Smith grabbed at the pile of papers as he fell and ripped the top sheet in half. The part that bears your very neat letterheads remained in his hand. He fell and more blood splattered on the floorboards. Not much, but enough. Either you or one of your men carried his body into the dark alley and dumped it there. When it hit the ground, the paper fell from his lifeless fingers.'

'But why would I even want to kill Hec Smith, Marshal?' The gambler could feel the hangman's noose around his throat as he spoke.

Cody Cannon did not hesitate for even a second. 'Because old Hec Smith had been supplying you with information concerning the cattle drives. You are behind the cattle rustling that's been plaguing McCoy.'

'But why would I kill Smith if he was supplying me with vital information?'

'That's easy; he caught whatever ails you. He got infected by greed. It's an illness that proved fatal.'

'But...' Barton tried to protest but Cannon interrupted.

'The bloody fingerprints on the paper I found outside are Smith's. I checked. I reckon that the ones on the top sheet of these papers will match his as well. Whether you rammed that knife into Smith or just ordered it done, you'll hang just the same, Barton.'

'Fingerprints?' Dick Hayes asked as he walked up to the marshal's side. 'What the hell are fingerprints, Cannon?'

Cody Cannon put the sheets of paper back into the brown-paper bag and then slid it into his deep pocket.

'Something that the dudes back East have come up with. They got the idea from England, I think. It seems that no two men have the same fingerprints and they're all different.'

Before the still-confused sheriff could say another thing, he and the marshal felt the weight of the heavy desk chair hitting them.

Madison Barton had moved quickly when he had spotted that both men were not concentrating on him for the first time since they had entered the Diamond Garter. He had lifted and thrown the chair over the wide desk and then drawn his gun.

Bullets rained across the room. Both lawmen fell to the floor as the sound of breaking glass filled their stunned ears.

Cannon pushed the chair off him and then scrambled to his feet with Hayes a few seconds behind him.

'He jumped through the window!' the sheriff exclaimed.

'Well spotted, Sheriff.' Cannon wiped the blood from his nose on the back of his sleeve. He drew one of his Peacemakers from its holster and unlocked the door to the alley.

As both lawmen rushed out into the alley, they were bowled over by Barton atop a large brown gelding. They crashed into the wooden walls as the hoofs of the startled animal passed within inches of them.

Cannon fired.

'Ya missed the bastard,' Hayes said.

'Which way's he heading?'

'South.'

'Quick,' the marshal shouted before hauling his companion up off the ground. 'We gotta get to the livery stables. I reckon he must be headed to Deadman's Fork where the rest of his gang are waiting for the Bar 10 herd.'

The sheriff raised a finger to his lips. 'That's the first time I seen Barton riding a horse, Cannon. Is that a clue?'

'C'mon, ya idiot,' Cannon shouted.

Dick Hayes ran after Cody Cannon in the direction of the livery stables. He still had no idea what was going on.

SEVENTEEN

Gene Adams had been itching to get to his feet ever since the rustler had first made his presence known. The rancher's hands were only inches away from the pair of gold-plated Colts that rested in his holsters, but he knew that they might as well be a thousand miles away. The owner of the Bar 10 ranch was kneeling, gloved hands on knees, staring straight into the barrel of Sam Flint's rifle.

Adams knew that there was no way that he could move fast enough to avoid being hit by the Winchester bullet that would spew out of the barrel, if he were to even try.

'How long do ya reckon it'll take for that old-timer to get your boys to drive the herd into Deadman's Fork, Adams?' Flint asked.

'By the sound of it, the herd has gotten a tad mean,' Adams retorted.

Flint screwed his eyes up and looked at the noisy herd.

For more than five minutes Adams had been studying the face of the horseman above him. He had seen the man before but could not recall where.

'Have we ever met, stranger?'

'Not socially, *amigo*.' Flint spat at the rancher and laughed.

The noise on the range was growing louder and louder. Adams glanced sideways and looked at the dust that was rising from the restless herd. He knew that the rider had made a vital mistake by shooting at Johnny. Flint had inadvertently lit a fuse that would explode sooner or later and probably claim a lot of lives when it did.

For the one thing that longhorn steers did not like was sudden noise. Their instinct was to try and flee and God help anyone who got in their way.

'What's wrong with them beeves?'

'That shot of yours spooked my herd, stranger,' Gene Adams said. He raised his hands above his head and straightened up to his full height. 'There ain't no way that my boys can handle them once they start stampeding. And they look pretty close to it.'

Flint tilted his head and observed the hundreds of cattle that were charging around on the range.

'Why don't them cowboys settle them

down, Adams?'

Adams continued watching the rifle barrel. He had noticed that it swayed when Flint looked towards the herd. It was only a few inches, but more than enough for the rancher to take advantage of.

'Longhorns ain't like white-faced steers. They get nervous and go loco,' Adams said. 'They're just plain ornery.'

Sam Flint did not know enough about the legendary longhorns to know whether the rancher was telling him the truth or just spinning him a line. He was used to rustling cattle but knew nothing about them except what they were worth to the gold-miners over in the territories.

'I thought that the Bar 10 riders were the best cowboys in Texas, Adams.'

'Not without me telling them what to do, they ain't.'

Flint tried to concentrate on the man standing before him with his arms aimed in the air, but his curiosity kept dragging his eyes to the range.

That was all Adams had been waiting for. Adams took his chance.

The rancher leapt forward and grabbed the barrel of the Winchester. He tugged it with all his strength. The rider flew over his head and landed behind him. Adams spun around and moved towards the man, who was rising off the ground.

Flint blocked a right cross and smashed a left hook on to the chin of the rancher. Adams reeled round as Flint charged into him. Both men fell and hit the hoofs of Flint's startled horse but they did not stop fighting. The punch that lifted Flint off Adams was a short right jab that sent the head of the rustler twisting sideways.

Blood trailed from Flint's mouth, then he staggered to his feet a fraction of a second after the rancher. Two more blows from Adams sent the rustler backwards until his spine hit the wall of boulders. But Flint was not finished yet; he had the deadly stiletto still hidden up his right sleeve.

As Adams charged at him, he allowed the

long blade to slip from his sleeve until it was in his hand. He lunged at the rancher, causing Adams to duck.

Stunned, Flint moved away from the rocks with the knife held at arm's length keeping Adams at bay. Then just as the rustler reached his horse, Gene Adams kicked the knife out of his hand.

Sam Flint spat blood into the face of the approaching rancher, causing him to stop in his tracks. Flint grabbed his rifle off the ground and threw himself on to his saddle.

Flint cocked the Winchester.

The Bar 10 rancher heard the sound of the deadly rifle being primed and although he was still blinded from the bloody spittle, Adams decided to draw. His black-gloved hands found the grips of the golden guns and drew them from their holsters. The Colts fired up at the horseman.

Flint felt the heat of a bullet hitting him high in his left shoulder. He squeezed the trigger of the cocked Winchester. The rifle kicked and blasted.

Gene Adams reeled on his heels as the horse reared up in front of him. Before he could get out of the way, the hoofs came down on the rancher's raised left arm. He tumbled backwards and hit the ground hard.

Somehow, Adams fired again.

As Flint steadied his mount he felt the rifle slipping from his grip. He looked at his shoulder and saw the blood pumping from the horrific wound in his shoulder, all down his shirt.

Then both men's attentions was drawn to the noise that had grown even louder on the range before them. Their gunshots had started the cattle running. They were now in full flight and heading straight towards the two men.

Adams managed to get back to his feet.

He had holstered one of his golden Colts when he suddenly heard the venomous cries of the rustler as the horse was hauled around and mercilessly spurred. Flint galloped back towards the canyon pass and his waiting gang.

Gene Adams had no time to think. He only had time to try and save his own life. He rested his back against the boulders and looked around for his chestnut mare. She was only a few yards away, standing tall and defiant against the hundreds of crazed cattle that were bearing down on her master.

'C'mon, girl,' Adams called to the alert mare.

The rancher forced himself away from the ridge wall and staggered to the waiting mount. He grabbed the saddle horn and urged the animal to start running.

It did.

With the same agility that he had honed to perfection over four decades earlier, Adams swung up on to his saddle and forced the horse on and on.

The mare thundered after the fleeing Sam Flint with a turn of speed that should have been beyond the exhausted creature but was not. With every stride of the long legs, the chestnut gained on the smaller mount.

Adams glanced to his left. The herd was gaining on him and showing no sign of turning.

Then he saw the golden pistol still in his right hand. He aimed over the heads of the approaching steers and fired one shot after another until the gun was empty. Only then did he holster the weapon, grip his reins in both hands and steer the mare away from the growing cloud of dust.

Had his shots frightened the longhorns?

Adams had no idea. He just stood in his stirrups and continued riding through the tall dry brush that edged the range. Harder and harder the rancher forced the chestnut mare on. Now dust was everywhere, covering everything. The dust off Flint's mount made it impossible for the rancher to see ahead and the stampeding herd to his left could now no longer be seen, only heard, as their dust billowed over him.

Gene Adams hauled back on his reins and held the mare in check. His eyes sought in all directions as he tried to find a safe place to steer his faithful mount.

There seemed to be none.

The sound of the stampeding herd was now deafening.

EIGHTEEN

Gene Adams was trapped by his own stampeding herd. He had never been afraid of the steers that he had bred until now. Now he was facing them with nowhere to hide and he knew that in their frenzied fear they would destroy anything in their path.

Even him.

Adams dragged his reins up to his chest and forced the mare to back up to the wall of boulders. The dust was now choking him, but it was the sound of the rampaging cattle that chilled him to the bone.

Suddenly the desperate rancher looked down and saw the dry brush that was the only thing between himself and the approaching longhorns. Frantically his fingers searched his pockets until he found a box of matches.

Without pausing to think, he dismounted, struck one of the matches and tried to light the brush. The clouds of dust blew the match out instantly.

'Damn!' Adams snarled, tossing the match away. Sweat trailed down his face as he vainly tried again.

Time was running out fast and the silver-haired rancher knew it. The ground was shaking violently beneath him as his gloved fingers withdrew a third match. He gripped it between his teeth.

Adams could feel his heart racing as he loosened the drawstring on his ten-gallon Stetson and dropped it on to the ground before him. He grabbed handfuls of the brush with his gloved hands and stuffed it into the hat before lying down on his belly. Adams took the match from his teeth and then got as close to his ten-gallon hat as possible before striking it.

This time the flame was shielded from the fast-blowing dust clouds by the large brim of his hat.

Adams watched as the fire caught hold of the brittle brush inside his Stetson. Gently he blew on to the flames. Soon the hat was ablaze. The rancher tore his bandanna from his neck and allowed it too to catch fire. He then quickly began to spread the fire into the brush that faced him and stretched away in both directions.

Within seconds the flames had spread through every scrap of tinder-dry brush that faced him.

Gene Adams grabbed his saddle horn again, mounted the curious mare and guided it back towards the wall of solid rock boulders. There was only a matter of ten feet between the horse and the fire. The intense heat began to burn both horse and rider, but neither noticed.

All they could concentrate on was the sound of the wailing steers somewhere beyond the smoke and flames as the ground shook with increasing ferocity.

'Steady, girl,' the Bar 10 man soothed the skittish horse.

Then it happened.

A dozen crazed steers suddenly broke through the smoke and blazing brush and crashed into the wall of gigantic boulders beside the horseman. Then they noisily continued on into the fire before disappearing once again into the clouds of dust.

As his gloved hands gripped at his reins, more longhorns smashed into the rockface only inches away from the startled chestnut mare. The sunlight flashed across the horns of the crazed beasts, forcing the rider to pull the head of his mount as far back as he could.

He knew the damage that those deadly horns could inflict.

Then, as the sheer volume of cattle increased, the smoke rose off their hoofs and was kicked into the sky.

For the first time for minutes, Adams

could see his herd. It was turning away from the flames and charging back towards the freedom of the open range.

The rancher suddenly felt an over-whelming sense of relief. He had somehow survived.

By setting the brush alight, Gene Adams had managed to turn the best part of the out-of-control herd away from him.

The rancher watched as the dust before and around him was finally swept away. The sight that met his eyes then made his heart skip a beat.

Above him in the crags he could see at least a dozen rifle barrels jutting out. He rubbed the neck of the chestnut mare and tried to keep her calm until the brush fire had finally burned itself out.

His eyes screwed up and stared out across the bright range at his Bar 10 cowboys. They had remained in their saddles behind the chuck wagon, waiting for the chance to try and ride out and control the rampaging longhorns.

He knew that his place was with the men, but Gene Adams wondered what chance he had of reaching them at the distant chuck wagon without being shot off his saddle. He swallowed hard and knew that there was no way anyone could outride a volley of Winchester bullets, however gallant their mount might be.

Adams rubbed his chin with his gloved fingers. He knew that he had to do something to try and resolve this deadly situation. If he did not, Johnny might try and do something daring but ultimately foolhardy.

There was only one thing in his favour, the dry-gulchers had not noticed him amid the dust and smoke. Adams pulled hard on his reins again and backed the mare up enough to turn her away from the mouth of the pass. He spurred the chestnut and galloped back towards the place where he had fought so doggedly with Sam Flint only five minutes earlier.

The rancher had a plan.

A blood-soaked Sam Flint had barely slid from his mount when Bodine Bonny came rushing down from the rocky crags carrying his rifle in his hand. The men who had been hired by the outlaw gathered around the dishevelled figure in disbelief. Flint looked more dead than alive, and probably was.

'What happened, Sam?' Bonny asked. The ashen-faced figure staggered towards him, then collapsed on to his knees.

'Gene Adams is out there some place. I had the drop on him but that damn herd went loco and I let him do this to me.' Flint gasped as he accepted a canteen of cold water.

Bonny gritted his teeth and glared out at the dust rising from the hundreds of cattle that had returned to the range after coming face to face with the wall of fire that the Bar 10 rancher had set. The fire had almost burned itself out, but the herd was now miles away.

'What the hell is Adams doing here?' Bonny asked.

Flint swallowed some water and shook his head. 'I ain't got no idea. But he is here and he's tough.'

The men all around the pair of rustlers began to talk amongst themselves. They headed slowly towards their horses. To them, it was over.

'Where ya going?' Flint tried to shout but the pain in his shoulder muffled his voice.

'We ain't hanging around here,' one of the men replied. 'The game's up. They know that we're here and they ain't gonna let us get our hands on them steers, Sam.'

Bodine Bonny cranked the mechanism of his Winchester and stepped forward towards the men who were already half-way to their mounts.

'The job ain't over 'til Sam says its over, boys,' he shouted. 'Now get back on them crags or I'll start shooting.'

The men stood facing the angry rifleman. Some were set on defying the man whilst others were too afraid to cross the stony-faced rustler.

'Make up ya minds, boys.' Bonny raised the rifle to his shoulder and aimed at the men before him. 'Them steers are worth thousands of bucks and all we gotta do is ride out there and round them up.'

Another of the men stepped closer to Bonny. He was a skilled wrangler but no gunfighter.

'It ain't as easy as it seems, Bodine. Them's longhorns and take a lot of skill to handle.'

'There are more of us than Adams hired to drive them to McCoy,' Bonny said coldly. 'We only got to ride out there and get them.'

'What if Adams and his men try to stop us?' another of the men asked.

'Look, Flint hired you boys. Some of you are wranglers and the rest are gunfighters,' Bonny stated. 'The cowboys round up the steers and the gunfighters make sure that we don't get no trouble from any of them Bar 10 varmints.'

Suddenly a weak voice came from behind Bonny. It was Sam Flint, who was leaning on a boulder pointing out at the range.

'Look, Bodine. Them damn Bar 10 cowboys have circled the herd and calmed the critters down. They've done our job for us.'

Bonny lowered his rifle. He stepped beside the badly wounded Flint and gasped in amazement. It was true. The Bar 10 riders had ridden out from the safety of their chuck wagon and used the longhorns' confusion at coming up against the brush fire to circle the now tired cattle and chase them until they became too exhausted to continue running. Johnny Puma and his crew had managed to regain control of the 500 head.

'Damn. They are good at their job and no mistake, Sam,' Bonny said. 'I'd have thought that it was damn near impossible to stop that stampede for another couple of hours yet.'

Flint nodded. He turned and pressed his hand against the wound. He could feel his heart beating against his wrist as blood trickled through his fingers.

'We got them licked, Bodine.'

It was a surprised Bonny who looked at Flint. 'What ya mean, Sam?'

Somehow Flint smiled. 'They've gotta bring that herd through the pass. There ain't no other way of reaching McCoy, Bodine.'

Bonny grunted in agreement and then looked at the men in front of him. They were a cold-hearted bunch who, he knew, would turn on their own mothers to make a few dollars. But they were still standing there and had not continued to go for their horses. Was it fear of his Winchester or simply greed? Bodine Bonny wondered to himself.

'Get back to your positions, boys. Sam reckons that them Bar 10 boys will have to bring them valuable steers through here after all. When they do, we'll have us a turkey-shoot.'

The rustlers made their way back up both sides of the canyon walls to resume their positions.

Flint spat at the ground. 'I reckon that Johnny Puma will try and drive them through here darn fast, Bodine.'

Bonny nodded. He watched their hired men priming their weapons in the crags high above them. He then looked at the pale-faced Flint and knew that he needed sewing up real bad.

'That wound is gonna do for ya if'n ya don't get to a doctor, Sam. That bullet has to be cut out.'

'Ain't no need. It went straight through.'

'Ya still hurt bad.'

'I'll last until we get them cattle into the territories.'

Bonny stared out at the range again as a thought suddenly struck him.

'What happened to Adams?'

'I ain't sure.' Flint sighed heavily. 'He shot me but I thought that I managed to shoot him as well. I know that he was on my tail when I hightailed it back here. Them steers were coming in real fast off the range. I only just managed to make it into the pass before they reached the ridge wall.'

'So Adams was behind you when them longhorns cut in on ya trail?' Bonny began to smile.

'What's so funny?' Flint asked.

'Could he have been trampled to death by his own herd?' Flint glanced at the range.

'There ain't no sign of the bastard. I reckon you could be right, Bodine.'

Both men began to laugh.

NINETEEN

Johnny Puma rode alongside Larry Drake and Tomahawk until the last of the exhausted steers eventually came to a halt. The three cowboys looked across at their comrades who were spaced out around the now stationary longhorns and all gave a sigh of relief.

The aged Tomahawk stood in his stirrups and raised a hand to his eyes to shield them from the bright sunlight. He was trying to see if his oldest friend had survived but everything was a blur.

'Can ya see Gene, boys?' Tomahawk asked the cowboys beside him. There was a panic in the voice that neither of his friends had heard before.

Johnny rested his wrist on his saddle horn and tried to see the familiar chestnut mare somewhere off in the distance. He knew that if he could see Gene's horse, he would probably be able to spot the rancher too.

Hard as the trail boss tried, Johnny could not locate any sign of his friend along the entire length of the ridge. The heat haze that rose between the herd and the three riders made it impossible.

'I can't see him, Tomahawk,' Johnny reluctantly admitted.

Larry rubbed the dust from his face with the tails of his bandanna and shrugged.

'Me neither. If he's out there, I can't see him, boys.'

Tomahawk went suddenly quiet. He

pulled his reins to the side and tapped his spurs until the black gelding began to walk back in the direction of the chuck wagon.

Happy Summers rode his buckskin quarter horse up to the two thoughtful cowboys and reined in.

'What's wrong with Tomahawk, Johnny?' the exhausted rider asked.

Johnny Puma gave a huge sigh. 'He's kinda upset about Gene, I reckon.'

'Do you think that Gene is still alive, Johnny?' Happy asked, keeping one eye on the herd.

Johnny turned his pinto pony and aimed the animal at the distant rocks. He could still see the sun glinting off the barrels of the Winchesters near the pass to Deadman's Fork. He knew that if he were to attempt to ride in search of the rancher, they would open up on him again. There was no way he was going to risk that.

One stampede in one day was enough.

'I ain't sure. If anyone could have survived out there when these steers went loco, Gene could have,' Johnny replied.

'Them rustlers are still up in the rocks waiting for us,' Larry observed.

'They'll have a long wait.' Happy chuckled until he saw the grim expression on the face of the young trail boss. 'You ain't thinkin' what I think you're thinkin', are you?'

Johnny tilted his head and raised an eyebrow. 'The cattle are under control, boys. You go and tell Cookie to fix us some grub, Larry. The boys need full bellies.'

Happy drew his buckskin mount closer to the thoughtful rider.

'You never answered me, Johnny.'

'I reckon that our best plan is to wait a couple of hours and then get this herd moving, Happy,' Johnny said.

'Moving where?'

Johnny was still staring into the heat haze, still hopeful that he might spot Gene Adams out there somewhere.'

'Straight down their throats, Happy. I'll make them choke on this herd for killing Gene.'

TWENTY

Gene Adams stood high in his stirrups and drove the exhausted mare on. The wall of massive boulders loomed high to his right as he eventually reached the place where he had fought Sam Flint so courageously. Every inch of the rancher was either bruised or bleeding, but Adams had no time to dwell upon his injuries.

Time was running out.

He had to try and get the better of Flint and his henchmen before they were able to use their weaponry on his trusty Bar 10 cowboys. The rancher hauled in his reins and quickly dismounted from the weary horse amid the dust that rose up off its hoofs.

Adams knew that the dry-gulchers had the advantage with their Winchesters. Few cowboys ever carried rifles when on routine cattle drives, and their handguns simply did not have the range of the high-powered carbines.

Gene Adams knew that the men who lay in wait for Johnny and the rest of the Bar 10 crew could pick off their targets without fear of any of the cowboys' bullets reaching them.

The rancher stared up at the wall of boulders and spotted a jagged rock protruding over the edge. It was at least thirty feet above him.

Adams plucked the rustler's Winchester rifle up off the ground where Flint had dropped it. It was still covered in blood. He checked it. It had ten bullets still in its magazine. He rested it against the ridge wall and moved across the sun-baked ground towards his horse. His gloved hands untied the saddle rope from the saddle horn and tossed it next to the rifle.

His plan was taking shape.

Once again, Adams leaned back and

looked up at the rockface before him. He sighed. It had been a long time since he had attempted anything as risky as this, but there was simply no alternative.

The silver-haired rancher spun round and then walked along the length of his lathered-up mount. He stroked its flanks and rested his hands on the saddlebags.

'This had better work, girl. I'm counting on you to do your part,' Adams muttered to the chestnut mare. He unfastened the satchel buckle and lifted the leather flap. He searched the bag's interior for something to write on and with. Then he recalled the battered ledger in which he had kept all his records of cattle sales for forty years. He raced around the tall horse and quickly undid the buckle of the other satchel. He raised its leather flap.

He found the battered old book and pulled it out of the deep bag. Adams tore out one of the blank pages from the ledger and pulled the two-inch-long pencil from the book's spine. He rested the paper on top of the book and then placed the book against the saddle as his tongue traced the tip of the pencil.

He wrote feverishly, then returned the ledger and pencil to his saddlebag. Adams knew that he had to secure the note to the horse so that it would be spotted immediately. His eyes searched the area around him where he had fought the rustler. He knew that the deadly knife he had kicked from his opponent's hand had to be close by.

Then his keen eyes spotted the sun dancing off the long blade. Flint's discarded stiletto was sticking out of the ground. He plucked it up, placed the paper on top of his saddle and rammed the knife through it into the padded leather.

There was no way that it would not be seen now.

Adams grabbed the ear of the mare, bent it towards him and repeated the name of 'Johnny' three times. He knew that the chestnut ought to be able to seek out and find the other Bar 10 horses out on the hot range. If it did, Johnny would get his note and, he hoped, not do anything rash. It was a gamble that he prayed would come off.

If it did not, the range would be stained crimson and littered with bodies before sunset.

Gene Adams slapped the rear of the horse and sent it galloping across the range in the rough direction of the distant riders. He knew that the chestnut would find his young friend.

When he had lost sight of his horse in the swirling heat haze, Gene Adams turned around to face the wall of gigantic boulders again.

The herd was now contained and subdued. Johnny had remained atop his pinto pony, circling the beasts, while his crew of exhausted cowboys had taken it in turns to visit the chuck wagon to get a bite to eat. The toll of being in charge of the herd and the responsibility that that meant was weighing heavily on his young shoulders.

Happy Summers rode his buckskin slowly across the dusty ground between the wagon and the herd. He had a large chunk of bread in his free hand as he steered the horse up to the pony.

'Ya gonna go get some vittles, Johnny?' Happy asked, crumbs flying from his mouth in all directions.

Johnny stopped his pony.

'I ain't hungry.'

Happy took another bite and then stared over the horns of their herd. Dust was rising in the heart of the heat haze. He pointed.

'Look, Johnny. A horse.'

The younger man swung his horse full circle and squinted into the bright distance. His heart began to race.

'That ain't just a horse, Happy.'

'Ya right!' Happy agreed, tossing the bread aside. He grabbed his reins in both hands.

'That's Gene's horse.'

Both riders thundered away from the longhorns towards the approaching mare. Johnny's fear that Gene was indeed dead grew with each stride of his pinto.

They reined in and Johnny grabbed at the bridle of the chestnut.

'Look, Johnny.' Happy pointed at the stiletto stuck into the saddle.

Johnny carefully pulled the knife free and stared at the scrap of paper. He unfolded it and began to read.

'It's from Gene, Happy. He ain't dead.'

'What's it say?'

'It says for us not to bring the herd anywhere near Deadman's Fork until he sorts out them rustlers.'

A frown creased Happy's chubby face.

'He ain't gonna try and take on them sidewinders himself, is he?'

Johnny licked his lips and handed the mare's reins to his pal.

'Take Gene's horse to camp and feed and water her.'

'What are you gonna do, Johnny?'

The young trail boss stared at the ground and the tracks left by the chestnut's hoofs.

'I'm going to follow these tracks back to

Gene. There ain't no way that I'm letting him take on that bunch of back-shooting critters on his own.'

Before Happy could say another word, Johnny had spurred his pinto pony and galloped away.

The gloved hands picked up the saddle rope from the ground and uncoiled enough of it to make a wide loop. Adams used his forty years of experience of roping longhorns and started to swing the cutting rope above his head.

But it was no steer that Adams was attempting to capture with the large twirling loop, it was the overhanging boulder which jutted out from the top of the ridge.

The rancher never took his eyes off the target high above him as his left hand fed rope to the ever-growing rope loop controlled by his right wrist.

Faster and faster the buzzing rope whirled around his head. Then, with his long-honed skill, Gene Adams released the grip on his right hand.

He watched silently as the rope loop traced upward through the air until eventually it opened up and secured itself around the protruding rock.

Adams wrapped the hanging rope about his wrist, then leaned heavily on it until the loop tightened around the rock high above him. He tugged it several times until he was convinced it would take his weight.

It had been many years since the rancher had asked his body to attempt anything as strenuous as climbing up more than thirty feet of almost sheer rockface. But there was no doubt in his mind that he would get to the top of the ridge.

He had to.

For Gene Adams knew that he had to make his way to a point above the crags where the dry-gulching rustlers were lying in wait for his herd and his men.

Adams tied the Winchester to the end of the cutting rope and gave the hot range a last glance. He wondered if he might be able to see the 500 longhorn steers once he reached the top of the awesome rockface. He pulled the black kid gloves tight over his hands and gripped the rope. He looped it around his shoulder, raised his left leg and pushed his boot against the smooth surface.

Slowly the rancher began to ascend.

The blazing sun beat down on his sweating face as he used every ounce of his strength to haul himself up the almost vertical slope. He missed the protection that the wide brim of his Stetson would have given him, yet it had saved his bacon by enabling him to set fire to the dry brush.

Adams stared up at the rock above him and the taut rope which was all that could keep him from falling before he reached the top of the high ridge. Then he realized that his boots were slipping on the smooth surface and that he was still ten feet from reaching his goal.

Taking a deep breath, the rancher pushed his feet off the rockface. He felt the rope tighten around him as he held his full weight on his arms and shoulders.

For more than a full minute, Adams just hung on to the rope until he was convinced that he could start to climb again.

He released the grip of one hand and stretched until he managed to grab the rope again. Then he did the same with his other hand. Hand over hand he slowly climbed until he was only inches from the dusty top of the ridge.

Gene Adams clawed his way over the rim of the rocks and lay there for a few moments. Then he hauled the rope up after him until he held the Winchester in his hands once more. He untied the knot in the end of the rope and placed the rifle against his leg, then he tossed the end of rope down to the floor of the range, so that its length was hanging from the jagged rock again.

Just in case he had to use it again as a means of escape.

Gene Adams cranked the mechanism of the rifle until it was primed and then began to walk across the top of the high ridge towards the men whom he knew were holed up in the far-off crags that overlooked the pass.

TWENTY-ONE

There was a desperation in the horseman who had fled from McCoy so suddenly. He knew that there was no future left for him in the railhead town. Only the gallows waited back there for the gambler now. For nearly two hours Madison Barton had ridden the stolen horse mercilessly.

He had to reach Deadman's Fork and the thirty men who relied upon the cash that he had generously given to Sam Flint. But the journey south was one that he was not taking alone. Others were hot on his tail.

Marshal Cody Cannon and Sheriff Dick Hayes were thundering after his trail, and had been since they had picked up their mounts from the McCoy livery stables. The land just south of the railhead town was almost flat and stretched for miles before the large boulders rose out of the fertile soil as if to warn of what lay within its canyons.

But the gambler held no fear of Deadman's Fork. To him it was sanctuary and the chance to make enough money for him to make a fresh start. For once, he intended being there when his band of ruthless rustlers struck. He would ride with them into the goldfields and ensure that he got his full share of the gold-dust that the Bar 10 herd would bring.

Barton had ridden at speed for some distance across the flat terrain towards Deadman's Fork before he spotted the two riders behind him. Then he had been forced to try and make his mount quicken its pace. But the horse he had stolen from behind the Diamond Garter was no match for the pair that were pursuing him.

Cannon's appaloosa stallion and Hayes' trim grey were gaining with every stride.

Barton had only one hope: to try and reach Flint and his hired men deep within the bowels of Deadman's Fork. He knew that if he could reach them, he would be safe from the two lawmen who had already marked his neck for the gallows.

Firing shot after shot with his Colt, Barton had tried to stop the men on his trail, but they continued to follow him. To his surprise, neither of the lawmen had returned fire. For, unknown to him, they had no desire to claim just his scalp. They wanted his entire gang of hired vermin.

Cannon and Hayes wanted him to do exactly what he was doing: to continue to lead them to where the rest of the rustlers were holed up.

The gambler drove his horse on and wished that he had spurs attached to his fancy footwear to encourage the useless horse beneath his saddle. For this was a mount that seemed never to have been forced to find its true potential before. If it broke into sweat, it would probably be the first time it had ever done so.

Madison Barton entered the maze of canyons and halted the useless horse long enough for him to take aim and fire the last of his bullets at the two riders close behind him.

Once again, his bullets missed their mark and the lawmen continued to reduce the distance between them.

Now he was afraid.

Barton dragged the reins hard to his left. He screamed at the horse and rode deep into the canyons. He had only been to this place once before with Flint. He knew where he was headed and hoped that he might get there before the herd of longhorn cattle entered the pass.

As he rode on, Barton suddenly became aware of the sound of horses' hoofs echoing off the walls of boulders around him. The pair of lawmen had entered the canyons.

TWENTY-TWO

Gene Adams moved like a man half his age across the top of the high ridge. He had made good time and knew that he was getting closer to the impending fight. The boulders grew ever larger the closer he got to the mouth of the pass. The rancher leapt over a six-feet-wide chasm and landed squarely on his boots; he paused to stare across the massive range. He knew that he must now be at least sixty feet above the surface of the sun-baked ground.

A mistake now could prove to be his last.

The sun was blisteringly hot, making the sweat run down into his eyes from the silver hair and burned skin that no longer had the protection of the wide-brimmed hat. He could feel the skin on his neck burning and knew that, in the cloudless sky above him,

171

the sun would only get hotter.

It was still only midday.

Adams scrambled up a smooth boulder and rested again at its top. This was the highest point of the ridge and he knew that he was only a matter of twenty or so feet from the edge of the opening to the pass. He placed the Winchester down at his side and pulled his golden guns from their holsters. He emptied the spent shell-casings from the chambers and replaced them with fresh bullets from his belt.

Adams holstered his guns again and pulled the small leather safety loops over the gun hammers to ensure they remained in his holsters. He lifted the rifle up and then saw the dust out on the eastern fringes of the huge range as Johnny Puma, astride his pinto, skimmed the desert on his way towards the ridge.

A wry smile etched the rancher's tanned face. He knew that there was no way that the youngster could stop himself from trying to come to the assistance of the man who had been like a father to him.

Adams wondered what Johnny would do.

He wiped the sweat from his eyes with his gloved right hand as he rose back to his full height. He carefully moved over the surface of the boulders and headed down to where he knew the rustlers were hiding.

Now he had to be even more careful. The men on the opposite side of the canyon walls might see him approaching.

He held the rifle firmly in his gloved hands.

He was ready.

Barton's horse galloped into the wide dusty pass and every one of the rustlers high above him turned and aimed their rifles down on him. Sam Flint had remained next to the long line of horses, watching his blood trickle out of his body between his fingers. Now he stared hard at the rider who dismounted.

Flint could hardly believe his eyes as he got to his feet and approached the dishevelled gambler who was staggering towards him.

'What the hell are you doing here?' Flint asked.

Madison Barton looked at the blood-soaked rustler and then started helping himself to his associate's bullets from the broad gunbelt strapped around Flint's narrow waist. Every bullet was sticky with the congealing red mess that was still pumping out of the shattered shoulder wound.

'I got me two lawmen on my tail, Sam,' Barton said, as his fingers tried to force the slippery bullets into the empty chambers of his .45.

Flint turned and shouted up at the men in the crags.

'We got two tin stars heading this way, men. A hundred dollars to the men who kill the bastards.'

Barton glanced into Flint's eyes.

'They know that Hec Smith was killed in my office, Sam.'

Flint screwed up his eyes and stared at the dust-caked gambler.

'How? Nobody seen me stick my stiletto into him. How could they prove anything?'

'Some real weird marshal turned up with Hays and nailed us to the ground with a load of so called facts. I didn't understand half of it, but he was about to arrest me.' Barton snapped his gun chamber closed and twirled the cylinder. 'I had to shoot my way out of town.'

Flint suddenly heard the echoing sound of the approaching horses. He signalled to his men before following the gambler behind a boulder near the gang's horses.

'If we kill them, I figure that I can safely go back to the Diamond Garter. With them lawmen dead, all evidence against us dies too.'

Flint pulled his right hand from his shoulder wound and rubbed the blood down his pants leg. He drew his pistol and cocked its hammer with his thumb.

'Then they're as good as dead, Madison.'

TWENTY-THREE

The appaloosa and the grey horse rode into the wide pass with more than thirty weapons aimed at them. Flint stepped away from the boulder and stared at the riderless mounts.

'What the hell is goin' on here?' he shouted.

Before Barton or any of the other men could reply, Cody Cannon and Dick Hayes appeared from over the top of the fifteen-foot-high boulder directly behind Flint and Barton.

Bodine Bonny rushed through a half-dozen of his fellow rustlers down towards the ground with his rifle gripped in his hands. He fired and screamed a warning with every step he took.

'Above ya, Sam. Look out.'

Cannon cranked the lever of his own Winchester and blasted three spirited shots at the large figure opposite him. Each shot found its target.

Sam Flint knelt and watched the lifeless figure of Bonny stagger and then fall head first off the crag. Dust rose into the air as the heavy body hit the ground solidly.

Flint fired his six-shooter up at Cannon.

Sheriff Hayes fanned the hammer of his Colt and riddled Flint with bullets.

Madison Barton suddenly knew what terror felt like. He tried to press his spine against the boulder behind him as if attempting to blend into the rockface and disappear. But there was no hiding-place from men like Cannon or Hayes.

The hired guns who were scattered across the two sides of the canyon walls returned fire as they descended towards the floor of the pass.

The men were evenly spread and made perfect targets for the two lawmen. Hayes used his Colt to shoot at those who were closer and Cannon took advantage of the fact that his rifle had greater range.

Bodies began to fall like leaves in autumn off the high rocks. The sound of dead weights hitting the ground echoed all about the pass. Gunsmoke trailed through the air from all directions as the battle continued.

It was a surprised Gene Adams who appeared high above all the fighting men. The rancher could see the gleaming stars pinned to the vests of both lawmen. He began to fire down at the rustlers who were trying to get off the rocks and reach their waiting mounts far below them.

Adams saw one man after another buckle and fall as he emptied the magazine of his Winchester. Bullets came back at the rancher as he slowly made his way down towards the heart of the bitter fighting.

Then his black-gloved finger squeezed the rifle trigger and found its hammer hitting an empty magazine. The rancher saw one of the rustlers clambering up towards him with his own rifle blazing. Gene felt the heat of the bullets as they passed within inches of his torso.

Without a second's hesitation, the rancher tossed his rifle aside, leapt from the boulder upon which he was standing and landed heavily on top of the rustler. Both men crashed on to the ledge and then rolled off the crag. Luckily for the rancher, he landed on top of the rustler as they crashed on to a jagged rock.

Adams felt the back of his opponent snapping beneath him. Then a volley of bullets rained at him from the opposite canyon wall from the handful of dry-gulchers that remained in one piece.

The rancher flicked both safety loops off his golden guns and drew them from their holsters.

With an accuracy acquired long before he had established the Bar 10, Gene started to pick off the men who were trying to kill him.

Cody Cannon raised his rifle to his shoulder, stared at the silver-haired rancher and aimed at him. Hayes grabbed at the long hot barrel of his companion's rifle and pushed it down.

'That's Gene Adams, Cannon. The owner of the Bar 10.'

'Lucky for him that you tagged along, Sheriff,' Cannon said. He spun round and started firing again at more of the rustlers who were emptying their weapons at them.

Another volley of bullets tore all around the rancher. Adams jumped down on to an even lower ledge and then found two more of Flint's men to his left. Before either of them could fire, he squeezed the triggers of his golden pistols and ended the men's fight permanently.

Knowing that there were now more men on the ground than were left in the crags, Cody Cannon slid off the boulder and landed a mere five feet away from the gambler. A bullet blasted from Barton's gun and ripped the shoulder padding of the marshal's jacket to shreds.

The lawman's rifle swung around and spat a bullet straight into the centre of the terrified Barton. The man staggered forward and smashed the barrel of his pistol across Cannon's face.

Cannon went hurtling sideways as more and more bullets came flying in at them from the remaining rustlers, who were still trying to get off the sun-baked rocks. The marshal hit the ground with blood trailing from the deep gash in his temple.

Barton looked at the blood seeping from the front of his white shirt and then gritted his teeth. He looked around and saw the tall appaloosa stallion standing in the shadows.

He knew that was his last chance of escape.

Dick Hayes suddenly saw a figure high above him and raised his Colt. He squeezed the trigger but the chamber was empty. As his fingers feverishly reloaded, he recognized that it was Johnny Puma making his way down towards the action.

Gene Adams holstered his left-hand gun and then knelt as he too was forced to try and reload the other weapon. As the shell casings fell from the chambers, Adams felt a rifle bullet passing within inches of his face.

Looking upward, his keen eyes spotted the last of the rustlers still alive on the crag directly opposite him. The man cranked the lever of his Winchester and then brought it back to his shoulder.

Gene tried to force bullets into the steaming chamber of his gun but knew that there was not enough time. He stared around the ledge that he was standing on. There was nowhere to hide. Nowhere to take cover.

Then he heard the deafening noise of two guns being fired from above and behind him. Adams watched the rustler fall forward and tumble off the high crag. Then he felt the impact of two boots landing beside him.

Gene tilted his head and looked up at the figure holding his two prized Colts in his hands.

'Johnny!' Gene sighed in relief.

'Who were you expecting? Tomahawk?'

The smoke was still drifting from the barrel of Madison Barton's pistol as he somehow managed to mount Cody Cannon's magnificent appaloosa stallion. The injured gambler could feel his life draining from him. Blood poured from the rifle wound in his midriff as he rode up and aimed his Colt down at the unconscious marshal sprawled out on the dust before him.

'Thought you were so damn smart, didn't you? Now you're going to die, Cannon.' Barton spat a mouthful of blood at the ground when he heard Sheriff Dick Hayes cocking his gun on the top of the boulder behind him.

The gambler turned quickly in the saddle, aimed and then squeezed the trigger. The sound of two shots rang out around the canyon pass.

As Barton watched Hayes twisting in agony above him he suddenly felt another crippling thud in his chest. The gambler tried to control the skittish stallion when he realized that he had been hit yet again. As the tall horse reared up and kicked at the lingering gunsmoke, Barton fell backwards and hit the ground heavily.

Madison Barton raised himself up on one elbow and pulled the gun hammer back with his thumb. He still had a score to settle and was determined to do so. Marshal Cannon rolled on to his side and stared down the barrel of the deadly Colt that was aimed at his face.

'You finished me, Cannon, but I'm going to make sure you don't live to celebrate,' Barton gasped as his bloodstained fingers toyed with the trigger.

Frantically Cannon tried to get up off the ground but was still too dazed to do so. He stared down the barrel of the pistol and heard himself praying.

The sound of the shot was deafening.

FINALE

It was a scene of total carnage. Blood was still running down the smooth boulders and soaking into the dusty ground as the bodies of the thirty men hired by Sam Flint lay scattered all over the canyon pass. Johnny Puma walked beside Gene Adams towards the stunned marshal who was staring at the body of Madison Barton lying beside him.

The bullet holes in the gambler's head were evidence of Johnny's accuracy with his matched Colt .45s.

'Did you do that, mister?' Cannon asked as the young cowboy helped the lawman to his feet.

'Yep,' Johnny replied sorrowfully. He walked over to help the wounded sheriff to his feet.

Cannon rubbed the blood from his brow

along the back of his hand and glanced at the tall figure of Gene Adams, who was watching his young friend.

'What's wrong with your pal, Mr Adams?'

The rancher sighed and rested his gloved wrists on top of his gun grips.

'There ain't many men as good with their guns as Johnny, but that don't mean he likes using them, Marshal.'

'He saved my life,' Cannon said.

'Johnny knows that, but it still leaves a bitter taste.'

The sound of horses made both men turn around and look in the direction of the vast hot range. Tomahawk and Happy reined in their mounts and stared in disbelief at the bodies all around them. Johnny helped Sheriff Hayes to the side of the still slightly dazed Cannon.

'What in tarnation happened, Gene?' Tomahawk asked.

Gene Adams shrugged.

'There was a slight disagreement here, old-timer.'

Cody Cannon helped the sheriff to his grey and watched as the winged Hayes mounted. The marshal then turned and stared at the men before him.

'What you men figuring on doing now?' he asked.

Gene Adams ran his gloved fingers through his silver hair.

'Tomahawk is going to get my horse and bring it back here and then we'll be heading into McCoy. I've got to buy me a new hat before my brains fry in this sun.'

'What about the herd, Gene?' Johnny asked the rancher.

'You're the trail boss, Johnny.' Adams smiled at his young friend. 'The herd is your responsibility. You drive them into McCoy when you're ready. OK?'

The youngster grabbed on to Happy's arm, then stepped into the stirrup and climbed up behind the wrangler.

'C'mon, boys. We got us a job to do,' Johnny said. The two horsemen turned their mounts and headed back towards the distant chuck wagon.

Gene Adams sat down on a boulder and noticed Cannon staring at him as he mounted his appaloosa.

'I've heard a lot about you, Mr Adams. I now know that the stories are all true. I'm grateful.'

The rancher smiled and then looked back at the range.

'I ain't nothing special, it's my riders. They all carry the Bar 10 brand.'

'I'll not argue with you, sir.' Cannon touched the brim of his hat, tapped his spurs into the stallion and began to lead the injured sheriff back to McCoy.

Gene Adams gave a gloved salute to the lawmen, then turned his head and stared back out at his men and the herd. To him, wherever he and his trusty friends were, that was where the Bar 10 existed. For whatever the Bar 10 truly was, it was branded into their spirits for all time.

This Large Print Book, for people
who cannot read normal print,
is published under the auspices of
THE ULVERSCROFT FOUNDATION